The Phoenix Girls

Book I - The Conjuring Glass

By

Brian Knight

JournalStone
San Francisco

Copyright ©2013 by Brian Knight

All rights reserved. No part of this book may be used or reproduced by any means, graphic, electronic, or mechanical, including photocopying, recording, taping or by any information storage retrieval system without the written permission of the publisher except in the case of brief quotations embodied in critical articles and reviews.

This is a work of fiction. All of the characters, names, incidents, organizations, and dialogue in this novel are either the products of the author's imagination or are used fictitiously.

JournalStone books may be ordered through booksellers or by contacting:

JournalStone
www.journalstone.com
www.journal-store.com

The views expressed in this work are solely those of the authors and do not necessarily reflect the views of the publisher, and the publisher hereby disclaims any responsibility for them.

ISBN: 978-1-936564-72-9 (sc)
ISBN: 978-1-936564-73-6 (ebook)

Library of Congress Control Number: 2012956362

Printed in the United States of America
JournalStone rev. date: March 8, 2013

Cover Design: Denis Daniel
Cover and Interior Art: M. Wayne Miller

Edited By: Norman L. Rubenstein

DEDICATION

To Norman L. Rubenstein, Godfather of the Phoenix Girls, and my own girls, Judi Key and Ellie Knight, who inspire me more than they know.

Check out these titles from JournalStone:

That Which Should Not Be
Brett J. Talley

Any Witch Way
Annastasia Savage

Vale of Stars
Sean O'Brien

Terovolas
Ed Erdelac

Twice Shy
Patrick Freivald

Limbus, Inc.
Anne C. Petty

The Devil of Echo Lake
Douglas Wynne

Pazuzu's Girl
Rachel Coles

Available through your local and online bookseller or at www.journalstone.com

ACKNOWLEDGEMENTS

Many thanks to my friends, in and out of the business, who have encouraged and believed in me, even when I didn't. Trent Zelazny, Monica O'Rourke, Jenny Orosel, Shane Staley, Larry Roberts, Tom Moran, and the many others. Special thanks also to Shawna, Judi, Ellie, and Chris.

Extra special thanks to everyone whose contribution added a little extra magic to this story – Christopher Payne, Norman L. Rubenstein, Jenna Meadows, M. Wayne Miller, Hannah Walthers, and Judi Snyder.

PART 1

Accidental Magic

Chapter 1

The Night the Magic Died

Four girls walked through the darkness, led by memory and moonlight to a familiar and secret place. They did not speak; the only sounds were the dry whisper of wind through tall, wild grass, and the occasional sob or sniffle as emotions peaked.

Everything had changed that night.

The echo of babbling water joined the wind, then overcame it, and the trail dipped into a darker valley. The canopy of a grove below was visible in the moonglow. The four girls' silhouettes vanished into the shadows of the trees.

Moments later there was a flash of light in the heart of the grove, and a fire lit it from within.

They sat on boulders circling the stone fire pit and stared into the dancing flames, determinedly not facing each other.

Then one of them did look up, a girl in her late teens with waist-length blonde hair, fresh tears streaming from her wide brown eyes. She scanned the down-turned faces of her friends.

"It's our fault. We should have been there. We should

have known."

A second girl, tall and athletic, with bright green eyes and thick auburn hair jerked her head up, glaring. "It's not our fault! She could have asked us for help, but she didn't. We would have gone. We would have helped her."

The third, a mousey girl with brown hair and small brown eyes nestled behind thick glasses said, "She was trying to protect us. She felt responsible for us, because ..."

"I don't need protecting," the second girl said. Her face was wild with anger, feral in the firelight.

The fourth, sitting furthest from the fire and hidden in shadow, spoke. "Stop it! Stop fighting. You're only making it worse."

"Can it get any worse?" the blonde girl asked.

A moment of silence followed her question.

"It's getting weaker," the fourth girl said. "I can hardly feel it."

"That's what he wanted," the auburn-haired girl said. "Break the circle, kill the magic."

The blonde girl rose and paced in front of the fire. "What are we going to do?"

The auburn-haired girl stood and reached inside her jacket, pulling out a slender, wooden wand. Its tip sparkled crimson in the flickering firelight. She gripped it in both hands, and snapped it in half.

"We let it die," she said. "I've lost too much tonight. Besides, we owe a debt now. We have to live long enough to repay it."

"Yes," the others spoke as one.

One by one, they stood and drew their wands, snapping them in half.

"Hurry," the girl hidden in shadow said. "We have to get back."

The auburn-haired girl pulled a burning stick from the

fire and held it like a torch, lighting her way from the fire pit to the nearby creek. The others followed as she stepped carefully down the path to the water's edge, to the base of a huge old tree whose roots wound and twisted into the water. There was a long scar in the bark where lightning had once struck it, a deep, wide crack where one of its huge twin forks had sheared away. The auburn-haired girl reached into it, her arm disappearing to the elbow, and withdrew a small wooden box, like a treasure chest.

She handed her torch to the blonde girl, pulled a large brass key from her pocket, and opened the chest. Inside was a small, battered book, its hard leather cover worn and curled at the edges. She dropped the halves of her broken wand into the box, and held it out to the others, who did the same.

Finally, she drew a second wand from her jacket, and held it up to the torch light. "I can't do it," she said, her voice catching on the last word. "It was hers. I can't break it." She dropped it into the chest and slammed the lid shut.

Crying out with anger, she hurled the chest across the creek, where it bounced into the open mouth of a small cave in the solid granite wall, vanishing in the darkness. A second later the key followed it.

The girl in the shadows moved forward, as if to run for the thrown chest and key, then stilled.

"It's over," the auburn-haired girl said. "Let's go."

They all rose and turned to go, except for the fourth girl, the one in the shadows. She moved forward only a single step, and stopped. Another figure, tall, red-haired, and with a ragged scar running down the right side of his face from temple to jaw line, stepped from the darkness and stopped beside her. He looked down into her face, eyebrows raised.

She grimaced, turned back to the others, and drew a wand hidden inside her jacket. She pointed it at their backs and closed her eyes.

There was a flash of blinding white light.

Then darkness.

Chapter 2

Little Red

Penny Sinclair came out of the old nightmare in her usual fashion, jerking awake with a gasp and throwing a hand in front of her eyes to block out that blinding flash of light. Slowly she became aware of her surroundings, not a country grove in the dark of night but the back seat of a bus.

Even as reality asserted itself, the dream faded from her mind. As always, only the barest sense of the nightmare remained, and the knowledge that she'd had it many times before in the past four months. The four months since her mother died.

Penny lowered her upraised hand and saw strange faces, all turned toward her. Curiosity was plain in some expressions, irritation in others, but most regarded her with naked sympathy, even pity.

Except for Miss Riggs, who sat beside Penny with her nose pressed in an open book, as oblivious to Penny as she had been on the flight in from California. Miss Riggs responded to Penny's few attempts at conversation with terse, single word replies and impatient grunts.

Penny ignored the stares and peered through the window past her silent traveling companion. A passing car threw a glaze of brightness over the glass, and as it faded she found her own reflection, bloodshot green eyes, her long, curly red hair mussed from a day of hard travel, staring sadly back at her for a moment.

It was hard to believe she was hundreds of miles away from the city she'd lived in her entire life. The view through her window was achingly familiar. It could have been any of a hundred northern California roads she'd traveled with her mom.

The bus slowed as it passed a low, wild hillock, then slowed further as the wild grass blurred into a field of early summer wheat. Penny's California daydreams evaporated into her new Washington reality when a weathered sign passed in front of her window.

Welcome to Dogwood, Washington – Home of Harvest Days.

Penny closed her eyes, sighed, and when she opened them, they were rolling to a stop in downtown Dogwood.

"Welcome home," Miss Riggs said, catching Penny's eye. She watched her with a familiar, narrow-eyed scrutiny, as if studying a picture she didn't much like.

Penny couldn't muster the strength for a reply, could barely muster the effort to stand when Miss Riggs rose to her feet. Hugging the bag that held her last few possessions, Penny waited for Miss Riggs to step past her, and followed her down the narrow aisle.

They were the only two to exit the bus in Dogwood, and no one waited at the curb to get on. A few moments after Penny stepped down onto the sidewalk, the door swished closed behind her.

Penny watched the silhouettes of the passengers through the bus windows as it moved into the distance, wishing she were still with them, driving into the orange summer dusk for cities and towns unknown.

I could have my pick, Penny thought wistfully. *Anything but this.*

The bus followed Dogwood's short Main Street and turned with it in front of an elderly looking school building. Then it was gone.

"Stuck here now," Penny whispered, feeling small and lost. Moisture stung the corner of her eyes and she wiped them away before Miss Riggs, or the growing number of gawkers gathering at porches and storefronts, could see her tears.

"What?" Miss Riggs regarded Penny again with those sharp, hawkish eyes.

"Nothing," Penny said, and followed her to a rundown white VW Bug sitting alone at the curb a block away.

The woman arrived at her car a block ahead of Penny, and stood holding the passenger door open, tapping her foot impatiently.

Penny controlled the impulse to turn and run the other direction, all the way back to San Francisco if she could manage it, and walked a little quicker, sliding into the back seat of the Bug and cringing as Miss Riggs closed the door behind her.

"Little Red," Miss Riggs said unexpectedly, startling Penny from her thoughts.

"Huh? What?"

Miss Riggs did her sigh again, it was a sound Penny was learning to loath, at once theatric and weary, and shot Penny a cross look through her rearview mirror. *I don't know why I even bother trying,* her expression said.

"Susan says your nickname is Little Red."

Penny nodded, surprised, and a little irritated. Little Red was her mom's nickname for her, and no one else ever used it.

She didn't even know anyone else knew about it.

Penny was born prematurely, and had been small all her life. Her mom called her petite, which didn't sound like a bad thing to her. The kids at the group home called her pipsqueak, runty, or the ginger hobbit.

Little Red had always been just between Penny and her mom, and coming from Miss Riggs' mouth, it sounded more like an insult.

"I can't hear you nod, you know," Miss Riggs snapped, though she could obviously see her in the mirror. "The polite response would have been 'Yes, Miss Riggs.' A little elaboration would have been nice as well, since I'm *attempting* to get to know you."

Penny bit her lips, cutting off the first reply that came to mind, and forced as polite a response as she could manage once her anger began to ebb.

"Yes, Miss Riggs, my mom called me Little Red. I don't like other people doing it though." She ended on a sharper note than she'd intended, and decided to keep her mouth shut from then on before she got herself into trouble.

The silence held for a few minutes before Miss Riggs broke it again. "Susan is anxious to see you. She jumped through a number of hoops to get you out of that orphanage, you know."

All feigned friendliness had left her voice. It was dust-dry and sharp as a whipcrack.

"She didn't have to," the woman was quick to add. "She agreed to be your godmother when you were a baby, but she doesn't even know you."

Penny bit her lips again. She didn't trust her mouth at that moment.

"Susan is generous to a fault, and there never has been a shortage of people willing to take advantage of it."

Penny could hold her tongue no longer.

"I didn't want to come here," Penny shouted. "I didn't ask for my mom to die, and I didn't ask for anyone's help!"

Penny took a savage satisfaction in Miss Riggs' stunned expression. Her eyes were open so wide it looked like they might fall out of their sockets. Her mouth stretched so tight it almost vanished.

Penny knew she should stop, she was probably already in trouble, but she couldn't. The words kept flowing, bitter water from a broken dam.

"Who are you anyway? If Susan is so anxious to see me, why didn't she come get me? Why did she send you?"

For several tense seconds Miss Riggs offered no reply. There was no sound at all except the unhealthy-sounding rattle of the old VW Bug as it sped over rough country pavement.

Penny turned away from the pinched face reflected in the rearview mirror, two conflicting emotions battling in her head, making her want to scream. She was ashamed at her outburst; she didn't like other people seeing her lose control. But a deeper part of her relished the shocked expression on Miss Riggs' face and was not a bit sorry.

Penny watched the field outside her window. The orange dusk had deepened to a violet twilight. Downtown Dogwood was at her back now, though she could still see the school building when she craned her neck to look back. She hoped the ride would end soon.

"I am Susan's sister. Her older sister," she said, regaining her calm, if disdainful, tone. "Though she so seldom chooses to take my advice that it hardly matters."

"The reason I was blessed with the thankless chore of fetching you from the arms of orphanhood," she continued in that same dry, hateful tone, "was because she had to work today. Since I did not, she took advantage of my *very limited* generosity."

The car slowed, and for a moment, Penny thought the woman was going to stop and let her out right there, in the middle of nowhere. Instead, they turned a sharp left at a sign that read Clover Hill Lane and started up a steep gravel path. Penny ignored the pinched and frowning face in the rearview mirror and peered through the windshield, straining at her seat belt to see the climbing road.

Something red and furry leapt from the grass, landing on four legs in the center of the gravel road. It paused there as the twin beams of the car's headlights fell over it, and turned to face them.

"Look out!" Penny said, but Miss Riggs ignored her and drove on. Penny clamped her eyes shut, not wanting to see what would happen next, waiting for the fatal thump as the little car's bumper hit the animal, but the thump did not come. She opened her eyes again and spun in her seat, scanning the road behind them. The angry red glow of the car's rear lights revealed nothing. No dead or injured animal lay in the dust and gravel. No live animal sprang back into the grass to escape them.

Penny faced forward again, her heart still racing a little, and the house at the top of Clover Hill came into view.

Chapter 3

Susan

To Penny, who had only ever lived in apartments in San Francisco, the house on the hill looked like a mansion. It was two stories tall, topped by a peaked attic that towered above everything and regarded the wild countryside with a single round window like an eye.

Penny wondered how far she'd be able to see from that window. Their apartment in the city was on the ninth floor, but in a place where every building is tall, you can never see far. Penny determined to make an exploration into the attic, if just for the view.

She wondered if her mom, who had apparently grown up in this town, had ever viewed this same countryside from such a high place. As always, the thought of her mom brought her tears back to the surface, dousing her natural curiosity with grief.

Miss Riggs pulled parallel to a stone pathway that ran through a slightly overgrown lawn to the house's front porch, and Penny grabbed her bag, pushing the door open and sliding out onto the dusty driveway.

The Bug was in motion again almost immediately, giving Penny barely enough time to shut the door and jump back a step. With a single, quick wink of her brake lights, Miss Riggs descended the winding driveway, and was gone.

Penny lingered for a moment on the first stone of a path through the grass, taking a longer, more thorough look at the house. Absorbing the sense of this strange new place that was now, for good or bad, her home.

It was well aged, if not neglected, its dull white paint peeling in a few places. Shuttered windows were open on the ground floor, their curtains fluttering in the evening breeze. A light shone from one of the second-floor rooms, and Penny saw the silhouette of a woman through the drawn curtains. Then the shape moved away, and for a moment Penny felt very alone.

Penny shifted her view upward and regarded the dark attic window. It really did look like an eye, she thought, dark and watchful. It felt as if someone was watching her from that high window. Watching and waiting.

Penny shivered, but the sudden chill came from a gust of cool wind blowing over the hill, not fright. A year ago, that watchful attic window and the unknown darkness behind it would have frightened her a bit, but not now. She had changed a lot in the last four months, she realized. There was no fear, but her curiosity came back strong. She wanted to look down on the world from that high, dark place.

It crossed her mind that this curiosity was a bit morbid, but Penny decided she didn't care. She was allowed to have a few morbid thoughts.

Adjusting her view to the front door, Penny started down the walkway, toward a porch that spanned the entire width of the house, and two tall hedges that framed the steps. A porch swing swayed silently in the breeze, and wind chimes hung by the front door tinkled a discordant melody. The steps creaked beneath her as she climbed them.

Then she stood, bag in hand, facing a closed door that was far scarier than any dark attic could ever be. She felt more alone than ever, standing at the dividing line between her old life, and a new, unimaginable one.

The tears she'd fought hard against all day finally came.

Footsteps sounded from the other side of the door, and before Penny could lift a hand to wipe away her tears, it opened.

For a long moment they only stood and faced each other—Penny outside with the troubled ghost of her old life lingering at her heels—and the woman, her mom's childhood friend, staring down in such stunned amazement that Penny was afraid she'd simply tell her to go away and slam the door in her face.

Would Miss Riggs have left her at the wrong house just out of spite?

Then the woman smiled and spoke.

"You look so much like her. It's good to see you again, Penny. I'm Susan. Susan Taylor." She held out a welcoming hand. "Come in."

Penny did not take the offered hand, but she did step inside, and the caged feeling she feared did not come when Susan closed the door behind her. This place was not like the group home. This place was a real home.

She felt a peace in this house, and a strange familiarity—as if she had many pleasant, but forgotten, memories of it.

"She never came back to visit after the two of you left," Susan said, stirring sugar into a mug of heavily creamed coffee. "But she wrote a few times a month."

"Can I have a cup?"

Susan gave her an uncertain look. "Aren't you a little young?"

Penny only shrugged. Coffee was a newly acquired taste

for her, one she'd picked up in the group home. After a week's worth of sleepless nights in a strange bed, she'd gone through her lessons in a constant state of exhaustion. She'd started drinking coffee to stay awake during classes, and had grown to like the taste.

After a moment's consideration, Susan fetched another cup. "Cream or sugar?"

Penny shook her head, and accepted the mug with a word of thanks.

"No problem, kiddo." Susan resumed her seat across from Penny.

"How long were you friends?" Penny spoke more to fill the silence than any desire for Susan's childhood stories, though she was anxious to hear more about the past her mom never shared with her. She had heard her mom mention Susan's name more than once, but there was nothing in those passing referrals to suggest their friendship was anything more than casual.

"Since before we started school," Susan said. "We were best friends until she moved away."

Something new occurred to Penny, a line of thinking she'd given up long ago. Her mom's life before Penny was an untouchable subject in their home, everything from her long-past childhood to Penny's absent father. All she had known before the caseworker found Susan, Penny's unknown godmother, was that her mom came from a small town, and that Penny's grandparents had died before she was born.

She knew nothing about her father. The only evidence she had that the man had even existed was a single, grainy picture scavenged from an old photo album. Her caseworker could find out nothing about him. His name was even missing from her birth certificate.

Penny wondered just how much Susan did know, and how much of her knowledge she'd be willing to share.

"Penny?"

Susan's voice startled her, and Penny realized she had been on the verge of sleep, despite the coffee.

"Sorry, I'm just a little tired."

Susan drained her coffee mug in one long gulp, then stood and scooped up Penny's bag. "There's a room for you upstairs."

Penny resisted the urge to grab her bag from Susan's hand. She'd learned to guard her possessions jealously at the group home, even viciously when necessary. But she reminded herself that this woman was neither a bully nor a thief. For now, unless Susan gave her reason not to, Penny would try to trust her.

Their footsteps echoed up the staircase. A few portraits hung from wood plank walls on the landing, but the single bulb light fixture hanging high above offered too little light to make the faces out.

The second-floor hallway was long and narrow, with a window at the far end looking out on the night. There were three doors, evenly spaced, on each side.

"Five rooms and a bathroom up here," Susan informed her. She pointed to the far room on the right. "That's my room, if you need me. The bathroom is behind us on the right."

"Where do I sleep?"

Susan stopped halfway down the hall, and pulled a rope hanging from the ceiling. The creek of old springs sounded, and a sliding ladder descended from the attic door above them.

Penny followed her up the ladder, emerging into darkness, then blinked as light assaulted her eyes. When she could see again, she was surprised into a smile, her first in many days.

The dust of empty years covered every surface of the attic,

but other than that, it was not what Penny had imagined. Not a cluttered graveyard of dusty old furniture, cardboard boxes, and castaway cloths.

"Nice," Penny said, and she meant it. She climbed the last few steps into a fully furnished and decorated bedroom. "I like it."

"It could use dusting, but I did wash the bedding for you." Susan sat on the corner of one of two single-wide beds. "No one's used it for years."

A low cathedral ceiling arched above them, ten feet high at the peak. Cobwebs hung from the ceiling and wood plank walls like gaudy Halloween decorations. There were two small writing desks next to each bed, each with a lamp and low-backed chair, and a dresser at both ends of the room. The dresser closest to Penny's freshly turned bed held a clutter of photographs and other odd items.

Small round windows faced each other from between the beds, like eyes made of starlight.

"If you don't like it up here you can use the guest room," Susan said. "It's a bit plain, but …"

"No," Penny said at once. "I love it."

"I thought you might," Susan said, flashing a knowing grin. She stood and stepped past Penny, stopping short of the waist-high railing around the attic door.

"You should get some sleep. I take Sundays off, so we'll have the whole day tomorrow to get to know each other a little bit better." A pause, then, "I bet you have a hundred questions for me."

Penny nodded. She did.

"Good night, Little Red," Susan said, and though it was strange hearing her old nickname from the lips of yet another stranger, it didn't upset her as it had earlier coming from her crotchety sister.

"Good night."

Penny fell back onto her amazingly cozy bed, the thick

feather comforter feeling like a cloud after a day spent in cramped, uncomfortable seats. She pulled her knees up and slid her legs below the comforter, pulling it up to her chin as she settled back.

Comfortable as she was, Penny knew she wouldn't be able to sleep. There were just too many thoughts, ideas, and feelings clamoring in her head. However, only seconds after laying her head on the pillow, her eyes slipped shut, and she dozed.

Penny had the old dream again that night, but this time there was more. She was running in the dark, down a beaten trail through tall and fragrant wild grass. Running toward something, or away from it. She didn't know which; only knew she had to keep running. Run like she'd never run before.

Then something stepped from the grass and crouched in front of her, something canine, predatory. It was only a shadow under weak moonlight. But even as a shadow its posture was visibly tense, its tall ears twitching and its fur bushed out.

"I've been waiting for you," it said, and Penny awoke with a scream locked behind her clamped teeth.

The dream faded as she rose to full consciousness, but the fear she'd awakened with remained, and it seemed like a long time before she slept again.

Chapter 4

Home, Strange Home

Penny awoke Sunday morning with a jerk, arms thrown up and shielding her eyes against dawn's bright light. The morning sun streamed through the window across from her, and in its glow, even the dust motes were golden. Yet, amid the morning's bright blue and gold, a single image from her dream lingered.

She pulled her blanket over her face, closing her eyes and grasping at the dream image—the red-haired man with the scarred face—and a few moments later when the rest of her dream had faded as it always did, the redheaded man remained.

Penny threw off her blanket and scrambled to the edge of her bed, reaching blindly for her bag. She seized it, yanked the zipper open, and dug through her clothes until she had what she wanted.

The photograph of her mother and father bore signs of travel, creased through the middle and bent at the corners, but the faces smiling up at her were unmistakable. It showed a much younger version of her mom standing next to a tall man with wild red hair.

Penny's hair.

Penny's father, she had no doubt.

They stood close, his arm draped affectionately over her shoulder. They were a picture of perfect happiness, appearing to be very much in love. There was nothing in that timeless pose to suggest the heartache and abandonment to come.

She studied the man's face, comparing it to her remembered image of the dream man. It took only a few moments to decide they were not the same person. Close, the hair in particular was almost identical, but the man from her dream was older, with a wider jaw and an intimidating gaze.

Then there was the scar. Her father's face was smooth and unmarked.

It occurred to Penny that the dream man could be an older version of her father, but she banished the thought with a chuckle.

It was a dream, she reminded herself. *Just a stupid dream.*

She walked across the room to put the snapshot on the dresser next to the framed pictures, and froze. It slipped from her fingers, seesawing to the floor at her feet.

Standing amid the clutter was a picture of a girl Penny recognized at once. It looked a lot like her, though taller, and with dark hair instead of red.

She lifted the framed picture with trembling fingers.

Her mother.

Penny dressed hastily and rushed downstairs, the framed picture in hand.

"Susan?" She checked the kitchen, then the living room, which she had only viewed fleetingly the night before, then passed the open door of the empty bathroom on her way to a large utility room with a door that led to the backyard.

Penny could not find her anywhere in the house.

Penny rushed to the front of the house and pushed through the unlatched front door, stopping short of the porch steps in surprise.

A boy sat on the top step, watching Susan argue with a man at the far end of the driveway. His dress was so stereotypical it was laughable. He wore a black Stetson too big for him. Tilted to one side, it disclosed a mop of unwashed hair and a mullet that hung past his shoulders. His white western style shirt and blue jeans were dirty, and the soles of his black cowboy boots thick with what could have been mud or cow crap. He held a pocketknife in his right hand, gouging the top step with it, digging out splinters of wood.

He turned at the sound of her footsteps, looking startled for a moment, then only irritated.

"Hush," he said. "I'm *trying* to listen."

"Stop that!" She pointed at his knife as its tip bit into wood again.

He ignored her, watching the arguing pair intently until they wandered too far away to hear, then turned to her again, folding the blade and sliding it into his pocket.

"Who are you?" His attention turned fully to her for the first time, he sized her up and smiled. It was a look Penny recognized and hated, the smile of a bully singling out a promising new victim.

"I live here," she said, hardly believing the words as they left her mouth, surprised that she was already coming to think of the place as home. "Who are *you*?"

"I'm Rooster," he said, actually thumping his plump chest with a fist.

"My papa," he pointed to the distant man, "owns this town, so you better watch how you talk to me!"

Penny began to laugh, was helpless not to.

Rooster flushed, taking a step toward her, and Penny matched it with a step of her own. Bullies at the group home had beaten her up more than once, and she had beaten up a few of them. But even if she lost, she never let them intimidate her. She'd discovered that if you let them push you around once they would continue to do it—but actually fighting was more of an effort than most of them liked to make.

Guys like this Rooster preferred easier targets.

"Tucker! Come on!"

Susan and Rooster's dad stood in the driveway again, the latter's face red with anger.

Rooster—Tucker—shot Penny one last sour look and turned to join him.

Penny walked to meet Susan, turning to watch Rooster and his 'Papa' disappear around the side of the house.

"Who are they?" She stopped beside Susan and turned in time to see them step through the strands of a barbed wire fence at the edge of the small backyard, into the wheat field on the other side.

"Ernest Price and his," she paused, as if searching for the right word to describe Rooster.

"His son," she said finally. "Ernest is a local big shot and resident pain in the ..."

Susan censored herself again and regarded Penny.

Penny heard real venom in Susan's voice, and understood she could come to feel the same way about Rooster as Susan did about his dad.

"He's a farmer," Susan said in a somewhat calmer tone. "But most of his money is in real estate. Ernest Price owns most of the land around Dogwood. He owns a lot of the land *in* Dogwood too."

Susan took Penny by her arm and led her back toward the house.

"He owns the building my shop is in, and the lease runs out next year. He's trying to strong-arm me into letting him farm up there," she gestured to the rise of land behind them.

"He farms the seventy back acres in exchange for my lease, but he wants it all."

Susan sighed and released Penny's arm as she climbed the steps to the house. She didn't go inside, but sat on the porch swing, gesturing for Penny to do the same.

Penny slid a hand in her pocket, feeling the corner of the framed photograph, then withdrew her hand and sat down next to Susan.

"The field behind the house is yours then?" Penny was curious, but also concerned. If Susan and Ernest's business brought them together on a regular basis, she was sure to see more of Rooster.

Susan faced Penny, a curious look of speculation on her face. Then, reluctantly, said, "No, not really."

"Then he does own it."

Smiling, Susan shook her head.

"Who then?"

"If I tell you a secret, can you keep it just between the two of us?"

Penny nodded, feeling touched at the unexpected confidence.

Susan looked right, then left, apparently checking to make sure Ernest and Rooster had not returned to make more trouble.

"You own it," she said, then laughed aloud as Penny stumbled over her reply.

For several seconds Penny was incapable of speech. She swallowed hard to clear her throat, licked her suddenly dry lips, and tried again.

"I own it?"

"All of it," Susan said, throwing her arms wide to indicate the house and all the land around it. "It's all yours."

The next day Susan returned to work, and Penny faced her first day alone at her new home. Though the past four months had been a flurry of activity with social workers and the other kids at the group home, she had somehow felt *more* alone there.

Here, at her new home, it was almost as if she'd found her mother again.

"Why don't you come with me?" Susan asked a final time on the way to her car, an ancient Ford Falcon with chipped blue paint and a spider web crack in the rear windshield. "You can browse the books and check out the town."

Penny considered it briefly, but decided she wasn't ready to face Dogwood's strange geography and new faces yet.

The field behind their house was off limits, but that was fine with Penny. She wasn't ready for another run-in with Rooster or his dad.

The stretch of wild land in front of the house was wide open and inviting though. So as soon as Susan's car vanished down the winding driveway, Penny started walking, replaying the previous day's conversation with Susan in her mind again.

"It's all yours," Susan had said, and when Penny only continued to gape at her, Susan elaborated.

"This house, this land, has been in your family for generations." Susan draped an arm casually over Penny's shoulder.

Penny had to fight an urge to shrug the arm away. This kind of casual affection was a new thing for her. "How big is it?"

"Pretty big. You own as far as the eye can see behind the house, and in front," she pointed into the distance past the driveway, "all the way up that hill to Little Canyon Creek. The creek is the property line…everything past that belongs to the state."

Penny nodded, trying to hide her astonishment at finding out she owned the equivalent of a couple of city blocks. She pulled her mother's photo from her pocket and held it out to Susan. "I found this."

Susan nodded and took the picture from Penny's hand, regarding it fondly. "The attic used to be her room. I stayed in one of the second-floor rooms when I was about your age."

"You lived here too?"

Susan nodded. "My parents died when I was fourteen. It was a bad spring. A lot of rain and flooding. There was a landslide on the highway west of town. Dad must have seen it too late. When he tried to stop their car, he lost control and went in the river.

"There was no one to take care of me after that, so your grandmother took me in."

Penny turned from Susan and stared at her hands, folded in her lap. She was close to tears again, but they were not precisely tears of sadness or loss this time. There was a touch of the old sadness behind them, but mostly they were tears brought by empathy. Empathy, and strangely enough, hope.

Susan was like her, an orphan with no real family left apart from her sister, but someone had cared for her anyway. Susan had been where she was now, and understood her better than any of the social workers ever could have. Penny couldn't think of her as a mother, would probably never be able to, but that was okay.

Susan was more like a sister.

It no longer felt to Penny like Susan was letting her stay out of obligation—though she thought part of it was the repaying of an old debt—but because in a way, they were family.

"June, my sister, was eighteen and had her own place by then. She invited me to move in with her, but we never got along. I think she asked because she thought she had to, and she was insulted when I decided to stay with your mom instead."

"Miss Riggs?" Penny interrupted.

Susan nodded.

"That's why she doesn't want me here," Penny blurted, and immediately regretted it. She had resolved not to make an issue of her argument with Susan's sister, but now she had brought it up.

Susan seemed unconcerned and unsurprised by this.

"Sorry about that," she said. "I wanted to pick you up myself but I had to work. Owning my own business is a dream come true for me, but it means I get to work six days a week."

Penny nodded her understanding. Her mom had worked long hours and many weekends at the agency in the city.

"What kind of shop is it?"

"I own a bookstore," she said, "but I also sell stationery and office supplies to most of the other businesses in Dogwood. The bookstore would never survive without the office supply side."

Susan began to rock them in the porch swing. "Living here rent-free helps too."

Penny relaxed a little now that the conversation had turned away from Miss Riggs. She was more than happy not to think about Susan's nasty-tempered sister.

"Your grandparents died before you were born, so when Diana took you to San Francisco she let me stay as caretaker. I pay the taxes and take care of the place. She willed it to you," Susan said, "but I'm the executor."

"It's all mine?"

"Yes. Once you turn eighteen you're free to kick me out, but until then you just have to put up with me," Susan said with a wink.

"Did you know my father?"

Susan cringed, and the porch swing stopped abruptly as she planted her feet on the floorboards with a loud *thump*. A tense silence followed as Penny waited for an answer. Any answer.

"I wish I could tell you about him, kiddo," Susan said at last. She patted Penny's shoulder, rose, and strode back inside the house, leaving Penny alone to wonder what her father could have done to turn her mom, and it seemed her mom's friends, so completely against him.

Penny stopped walking at intervals to take in new scents, scents she'd never experienced in the city: wildflowers, dew-dampened grass, and acres of wild clover. She walked and walked, paying little attention to her direction. She heard the far off babble of running water, Little Canyon Creek maybe, but couldn't locate its source.

The mostly flat ground became sloped and rocky; the wild grass and clover thinned, stunted scrub brush and scrawny trees rose up to meet her. She was determined to gain the top of the hill—to look back and see her house from afar.

"Ehem." The sound of a cleared throat.

Penny jumped back a step, startled, and tottered until she found a handhold on a stunted tree twisting its way out of the ground to her left. She turned her head left, right, then peered down the slope behind her.

"Ah, my apologies miss. Didn't mean t' startle you."

Penny faced forward again and saw the owner of the voice at the top of the hill, only feet in front of her. A large red fox, sitting on its haunches, its head cocked to one side, and grinning down at her. Penny had seen foxes in books and on TV, but none of them had been this large. None of them had talked, either.

"Uh …" Penny said. "Wha …?"

"I wondered when you'd make it this way. Fancy a chat?"

Penny did not fancy a chat.

Shrieking, she let go of the tree and ran straight down the hill as fast as she had ever run, very lucky to make it to the bottom still on her feet. She ran until the big fox was a speck sitting atop the distant hill. She ran until the hill itself was an indistinct lump in the green distance.

Panting, Penny stomped up the porch steps, threw the front door open, and rushed inside, slamming it shut behind her and locking it.

Chapter 5

Zoe

The rest of that day and all of the next, Penny stayed safely shut in the house. She spent most of the time in her room, rereading one of her old books, which failed to hold her interest for more than a few minutes at a time, tuning her bedside radio endlessly in search of something that wasn't country music or talk radio, and staring out the small round window across the room from her bed. She could see the fox's hill in the far distance, and just past its crest, the high boughs of a grove of trees.

Sometimes she saw the fox, a far off speck moving in the distance.

When Penny had to go downstairs, she moved with speed, glancing cautiously through any window she happened to pass, seeing that weird talking fox more often than not. Sometimes it seemed to grin at her; sometimes it dropped a conspiratorial wink.

She thought about telling Susan, but couldn't think of a way to bring it up that didn't sound crazy. Besides, whenever Susan came home from work the fox disappeared.

On Wednesday morning Penny surprised Susan by meeting her at the door, dressed and ready to go into town.

"It's about time, kiddo. Jenny wants to meet you." Jenny was Susan's only employee. "You need to get out anyway. Try to make a few friends before school starts."

Penny mumbled a reply. Her stomach squirmed a little at the prospect of meeting new kids, trying to make new friends. She couldn't banish the thought that every kid in this small town would turn out to be as annoying and stupid as Rooster.

Nevertheless, Penny knew she would have to try eventually.

Even if she didn't manage to make any new friends, she might find something new to read at Susan's bookstore.

Most importantly, she would be away from the house for the day, in town, where she hoped the talking fox wouldn't follow.

It was a short drive from the end of Clover Hill Lane to downtown Dogwood. Penny looked out her window as they passed the school. Some younger kids played on the merry-go-round, slide, and jungle gym. The football field next to the school was empty, but Penny saw more kids, some her own age, in the city park on the other side of a tall fence. Most looked like they were just passing through, on their way to one place or another. But a small group of boys played baseball, and a girl sat alone under a tree close to an aged gazebo reading a book.

"She's new here too," Susan said, nodding toward the reading girl. "She comes in every few days to browse my books."

Penny did a double take at the lone girl.

"Can I go to the park?"

"Of course you can," Susan said, and smiled at her. "That's the advantage of small town living, kiddo. You can go out by yourself."

This was a new concept for Penny. In the city, her mom only let her out with the babysitter. So even though there was more to do there, she still didn't get to go out often.

Here she was free to go out on her own, and the enormity of this new freedom was a little shocking.

Dogwood, small as it was, suddenly seemed huge with possibilities.

"There it is," Susan said, pointing at a shop front with a blue awning and a sign that said Sullivan's.

Penny peered through the front windows as they passed, catching a glimpse of a plump teen, Jenny, she assumed, with thick glasses and short brown hair, turning on lights inside. She also caught a glimpse of the shop next to Sullivan's. The windows of that shop were still pitch black. The sign hanging above the door said: Golden Arts – Jewelry, Time Pieces, Minerals and Gems. At the end of the block, they turned down a side street and pulled into a parking lot behind the row of main street shops.

Penny followed Susan through the plain-looking back entrance, passed through a small storage area, then stepped into the shop as Jenny flipped the sign from *Closed* to *Open* and turned a key in the front door's lock. When she turned and saw Penny standing there, her face lit up.

"Well, you finally decided to come." She stepped forward and scooped Penny into an unexpected and awkward hug. "I was beginning to think Susan had an imaginary friend."

"It's nice to meet you," Penny said, forcing an uncomfortable smile as she waited for Jenny to let her go.

Penny let her eyes wander around the shop, taking in the aisles of shelved books in the back half. The front half was a less interesting maze of office supplies and stationery.

"Eyeballing the stock already," Susan said, moving behind the till and turning it on. "Diana raised a reader then."

Penny regarded her curiously for a moment, then understood. She was not used to hearing her mom referred to as Diana. "Well, I *can* read."

Susan turned to Penny again her eyes narrowing. "Oh, I see."

Penny felt like shrinking under the sharp gaze, but Susan couldn't hold the stern look. She broke into a smile.

"If you aren't a reader now," Jenny said, "you will be by the time we're finished with you."

Penny left Sullivan's an hour later with two new books under her arm—a compilation of classic ghost stories for herself and a fantasy story for the girl in the park. The lone girl in the park was as good a place as any to start *trying to make new friends*. They had one thing in common at least.

"Give this to her," Susan said, shoving the book into Penny's hands, "tell her it's from you and Susan at Sullivan's."

Penny walked down to the end of the short block, pausing at the crosswalk for several seconds before stepping into the street. She wasn't accustomed to light traffic and had to convince herself that traffic wouldn't materialize the second she stepped into the road.

She crossed at a run and made it to the other side unscathed. A look back over her shoulder showed empty blacktop in both directions, with a handful of cars and trucks parked along the main street. Somewhere, distantly, she could hear the sound of running cars, but the sound of shouting and laughing children in the park drowned it out a moment later.

She scanned up and down the street, checked the distant park and school playground carefully, but couldn't see the fox anywhere.

"Probably imagined the whole thing," she said to herself, and set off. But when she arrived the girl was gone. A small bag lay beneath the tree, but the girl and her book were gone.

A shout from the group of kids farther along made her look up, and Penny saw the girl standing in the middle of the group of boys she'd seen playing baseball. They had abandoned their game in favor of another sport.

Most of them stood in a rough circle, watching and laughing, while three of them threw her book into the air to each other, making her run for it, jump for it, but throwing it before she could get it back.

"Give it back!" She lunged for it as a boy Penny recognized held it aloft, jumping when her fingers brushed the spine, and throwing it to one of his pals.

Penny dropped her books next to the girl's bag and ran toward them.

The boys didn't see her coming until she was a few feet away. A few of them pointed and laughed.

"Who invited the leprechaun?" A tall, skinny boy leaning on his baseball bat like a cane smirked at her. She kicked the bat out from under his hand as she passed, making him stumble.

Rooster turned and saw her, his eyes going wide a second before the book sailed his way again, whacking him on the back of the head.

"Ouch!" Rooster shouted and turned to see who had thrown the book.

Penny reached up and grabbed him by the ear, giving it a twist and bringing him to his knees.

"Leave her alone," Penny said, giving his ear another twist when he tried to rise.

"Ouch! Let go," Rooster shouted, flailing, grasping at her long red hair.

"No you don't!" The girl, almost a foot taller than Penny, with long dark hair and deeply tanned skin, grabbed Rooster's arm and forced his fingers open, releasing Penny's hair. She twisted his arm behind him and sat on his back, forcing his face into the grass.

One of Rooster's friends stepped forward and Penny scooped up the bat, holding it in her hands casually and grinning. The boy stopped and gave her a wary look.

Most of the others simply stood around, looking amazed and amused at the turn of events.

Still holding the bat, Penny bent down and picked up the book.

"Let me up," Rooster said, his voice muffled by the grass.

"I think you should apologize first," the girl said, and gave his arm a twist. "It's not nice to pull a girl's hair."

"Sorry," Rooster shouted. "Oowee!"

Smirking, the girl let him go and stood next to Penny.

"Thanks," she said as Penny handed the book over.

"No problem," Penny said, still keeping her eyes on the boys around them.

"So," said one of the boys, kneeling down to help Rooster up. "This must be Susan's orphan."

"Yeah, so what if I am?" Penny glared at him.

The boy gave her a cold look and jerked Rooster to his feet by his armpit. "You better watch yourself, new girl. Both of you."

"Or what?" Penny and the other girl said in unison.

He only smiled at them.

"Come on, little bro," he said to Rooster, and led him back to their makeshift baseball diamond.

Penny threw the bat down and followed the girl back to her tree.

"Thanks. I'm Zoe."

"Penny," Penny said, catching up to her.

Already Dogwood was turning out to be more exciting than she had expected.

Penny arrived at the big tree just behind Zoe, who bent to pick up her bag, eyeing the new books in the grass. Penny picked them up and handed one to her.

"From Susan … at the bookstore."

Zoe regarded the offered book for a moment before taking it. "What's this for?"

"Susan thought you'd like it," Penny said—because *It's a bribe to make you be my friend,* while more accurate perhaps, was too embarrassing to admit out loud.

"Oh … thanks," Zoe said awkwardly. She tucked it under her arm with the other book and glanced around, as if searching for an escape. "Listen, I gotta get home before my grandma has a fit."

Zoe dashed across the street without looking, pausing briefly on the center line to regard Penny again. "Tell Susan I said thanks."

Then she was off again, sprinting down the sidewalk.

Penny stood alone at the edge of the park and watched Zoe disappear around the corner of the block, wondering if she'd done something to offend her.

A new silence made her look around, and she saw Rooster and his older brother watching her.

Time to go back inside.

Penny spent the rest of the afternoon in Susan's shop reading, and went home that evening feeling a little disappointed. For the few minutes they were together, giving Rooster a taste of his own medicine, it was like having a friend again, something she'd not had since leaving her apartment in the city behind.

She didn't see the fox at all that evening.

The next day she saw Zoe only briefly as the girl passed the storefront and rushed into the neighboring shop, Golden Arts.

"You should go check the rock shop," Susan said, noticing Zoe dash inside.

Penny shrugged, then shook her head and went back to her book. She was bored, but not so desperately bored she was going to start stalking the locals.

On Friday morning Zoe turned up about an hour after opening.

Penny watched with muted interest as Zoe approached Susan, her face pointed toward the floor and a cascade of long dark hair covering it.

Susan and Jenny noticed her too.

"Good morning," Susan said, setting aside the order form she'd been filling out.

Jenny waved, then went back to facing and straightening a shelf of binders.

"Hi, Susan. Thanks for the book." She glanced over at Penny, who quickly looked back down at her own book but couldn't pick up the dropped thread of her story.

"I hope it's one you like. I've seen you look at it a few

times."

"Yeah, it's really good." She stopped in front of Susan, finally looking up into her face. "I made this for you ... to say thanks, you know."

Penny snuck another surreptitious glance and saw Zoe holding out a small dreamcatcher. About the size of her outstretched hand, a dozen beaded strings crisscrossed a frame of slender willow. In the center, a clear crystal caught and reflected light from the overhead fluorescents.

"That's beautiful," Susan exclaimed, turning it back and forth in her hand to watch the reflected light dance in the crystal. "I'll hang it over the door."

"Thanks," Zoe said, and Penny saw a blush creep into her cheeks.

She turned to Penny next, and instead of looking away again Penny forced a smile. "Hi Zoe."

"Hi ... I brought you this." She held out an old and clearly well-read paperback book, a *Year's Best Horror Stories* that was older than both of them put together. "I noticed you like scary stories, so ..."

"It's great," Penny said, and meant it. Not the book—Penny thought this one looked especially cheesy, even for a book of horror stories—but that Zoe had brought it. Maybe what Penny had mistaken for snobbery was just shyness. "Thanks."

Zoe looked up then, even smiled. "You wanna go hang out for a bit?"

Chapter 6

The Fox's Game

Within the hour, Penny knew as much about Zoe as she ever had about any of her friends from the city.

Zoe had moved to Dogwood at the end of the last school year to live with her grandmother while her mom and dad pursued careers as over-the-road truck drivers.

"It's just for a few months," she said. "They'll get tired of it pretty soon and come back for me."

Penny couldn't help but notice that Zoe didn't seem completely convinced of this. She avoided Penny's eyes for a second, fiddling with a hole in the knee of her jeans.

"My dad's an Indian. For a while I stayed with my other grandma on the reservation, but I didn't like it there much, so they said I could come here."

"Do you like it here?"

Zoe shrugged. "It's okay, I guess. I like Sullivan's and the rock shop, but I don't have any friends here."

"Me either," Penny said. "I just moved in with Susan. She's cool, but my closest neighbor is that little booger with the mullet."

Zoe laughed. "Lucky you."

There was a nervous silence, the kind that grew harder to kill with every second it survived. Then, much to Penny's relief, Zoe ended it. "Have you seen the rock shop yet?"

"No," Penny said, glancing back toward the Golden Arts. The display window that had still been dark the only time she'd taken a good look in it, now glowed with bright fluorescent light.

"Let's go," Zoe said. "You'll love it…they've got the prettiest rocks in there."

Penny had to work to keep up with the taller girl's strides. Crossing the street halfway between intersections, Penny shot nervous looks up and down. The lack of morning rush-hour traffic still unnerved her.

They passed Sullivan's, and she saw Susan smiling at them through the window. They waved, and she waved back.

The bell over Golden Arts' door jingled, and she had to rush to catch it before it swung shut again. She found Zoe inside, striding toward an open door set in the far wall.

An old man behind the glass display counter nodded at Zoe and said, "Morning, Zoe."

Then his eyes fell on Penny, and he flinched as if goosed.

Penny gave a little wave, which he returned, and he watched her all the way through the showroom door as she caught up with Zoe.

Penny found Zoe standing at the end of a long table, pawing through a bin of loose stones. "What's with that guy?"

"Dunno," Zoe said, showing zero interest.

While the main floor of the shop looked like any other low-end jewelry store Penny had ever been inside, the smaller back room was a warehouse of rough gemstones, crystals, and strange minerals. Shelves crowded with displays of sparkling stones, opened amethyst geodes, great shining lumps of fool's gold, and interesting formations of unidentifiable crystals covered the walls. A row of display shelves dissected the room.

"Weird," Penny said, staring around.

"I want to be a geologist," Zoe said. "I love minerals and gems."

"You'll make a good one too," said the old man from the doorway.

He reached into the stone bin, plucking a handful of stones at random. "What'r these?"

Zoe grinned, and named them, one by one. "Carnelian, Jasper, Obsidian, and Turquoise."

"And this one?" He held up a blue crystal, Penny's favorite of the bunch.

Zoe, however, seemed unimpressed. "Quartz crystal. But someone dyed it to turn it blue, so it's not *really* blue."

The man laughed, dropped the stones into a paper bag, and handed it over to Zoe, whose grin returned.

"You win again," he said dramatically. Then he turned to Penny. "You're a Sinclair, aren't you?"

"Uh, yeah," Penny said, a little surprised.

"I knew it," the man said, snapping his fingers. "I have an eye for faces. Never was good with names, but I knew I recognized you."

"I've never been here before."

The man waved her comment away. "Don't matter. Family resemblance. I near jumped out of my skin when you walked in. You look a lot like your mamma."

"You knew my mom?"

Zoe quit sifting through the bins of crystals and polished stones, watching Penny and the old shopkeeper with interest.

"Oh, yeah," he said enthusiastically. "She used to come in here all the time when she was younger. Must have had quite a collection of pretty rocks, all the time she spent here."

He must have quite a memory, Penny thought. The excited flutter in her stomach intensified. Would he remember her father too?

"Your mamma, your aunt, and their friends were in here all the time."

Penny's hopes sank at once. She didn't have an aunt. The old guy might have a good memory for faces, but seemed confused about other details.

Still, it was worth asking.

"Do you remember ..." but Susan's voice cut her off as she stepped up behind the old shopkeeper.

"Penny, why don't you two head back to the shop? I'm sending Jenny out for a late breakfast."

Penny didn't know if she'd done anything wrong, but Susan looked irritated. Had Susan guessed what Penny was about to ask the old man?

"Thanks," Zoe said, grinning as she stepped past Susan into Golden Arts' showroom. She waved at the shopkeeper and said, "I'll be back later."

He nodded, keeping a wary eye on Susan as Penny followed Zoe out.

They waited outside Golden Arts for a few moments, but Susan did not join them.

"Come on," Zoe said, striding toward Sullivan's open door.

Penny took a step, and gave a little gasp, freezing on the spot.

The talking fox stood at the other end of the block facing her, unconcerned, as a small group of old women passed it on their way to the senior center, which had a banner over its door advertising All Day Bingo Friday.

A boy on a bicycle passed it a moment later, stopping to

scan the street before he continued toward the park.

Could no one else see it?

The fox's furry snout parted in a sharp-toothed grin, and it winked.

Penny ran to catch up with Zoe, pulling the shop's door closed behind her.

Penny sat next to Zoe on one of Sullivan's comfortable reading couches while her new friend cheerily recounted the story of their meeting. Zoe burst out laughing during the retelling of her favorite part, sitting on Rooster's back and making him apologize.

Susan, for her part, tried not to look too amused as she admonished them both, but wasn't able to hold the stern look she strived for. The corners of her lips kept quivering with a barely suppressed grin.

Penny, her attention split between the sidewalk past the glass front and Susan, nodded when it seemed appropriate, and promised at the end of Susan's halfhearted lecture not to beat up any more town boys. She was afraid that weird fox might just trot up the sidewalk and push through Sullivan's front door.

Slowly, Penny calmed down, silently telling herself that her overactive imagination had shown her the fox where a dog had been. That made sense—the people passing it wouldn't have made a fuss about a friendly neighborhood mutt—but she remained only half-convinced.

When Jenny returned, her arms loaded with a tray of Styrofoam cups and a box of doughnuts, Penny rushed to open the door.

Jenny caught sight of Zoe. "Welcome back."

Zoe waved, giving the doughnuts a hungry look as Jenny set them on the table in front of the reading corner couch. "Thanks," she said, accepting an Italian soda from Susan and grabbing a maple bar.

No sooner had Susan and Jenny gobbled down a doughnut each, chasing them with heavily creamed coffee, the business day started at Sullivan's. A half-dozen people, young and old, and even an elderly farming couple from out of town, browsed the shelves. The phone rang constantly, local businesses ordering office supplies, which Jenny would deliver later that afternoon.

Penny and Zoe stuffed themselves on doughnuts and headed back outside.

Penny scanned the street and sidewalk again, but there was no sign of a fox, talking or otherwise.

"Come on," Zoe tugged on Penny's arm. "There's an amethyst crystal in there I want to buy."

Penny had no real interest in spending the day rummaging through boxes of rocks, interesting as Zoe found them, but followed anyway.

The old shopkeeper met them with a wave, and a slightly embarrassed smile. "Welcome back, young ladies."

Zoe gave him a distracted wave as she honed in on the back room again, but Penny lingered, more interested in his memories than his rocks.

"I'm sorry to hear about your mother, young lady. She was a nice girl. You must miss her a lot."

Mention of her mom momentarily drove all questions from her mind. Just when she was finally thinking of something besides her mom, when it seemed she was able to go a day without crying, all the sadness crashed back down on her. Penny looked at her feet so he wouldn't see her burning eyes, so he wouldn't see how close to tears she was now, and said, "Thank you. I do miss her, but I'm doing okay."

He made a sound of affirmation, almost a grunt. "Miss Taylor is the nicest person you could have found to stay with.

She'll take care of you."

Penny nodded, then hurried to the back room, questions about her father forgotten for the time. She found Zoe standing over the same bin as before eyeing the polished stones like the contents of a treasure chest.

"Ah ha!" She pulled a cluster of fat purple crystals from the bin and held them up for Penny to admire, then rushed past her to pay for them.

Oh well, Penny thought, giving her shoulders a shrug. *So what if she's a bit weird.*

Everyone was weird in some way. At least Zoe was weird in a fun way.

Rooster, his brother, and the rest of the boys were back at the park for their daily ball game, so Penny and Zoe decided to walk over to the school and have a look around. As they passed the game in progress, Zoe stopped and said, "Look at that!"

Penny turned and saw the fox again, sitting in the outfield, watching the game.

"You … you can see it too?"

Zoe gave her an incredulous sideways glance and said, "Of course I can."

However, when the fox rose on all four legs and trotted

into the infield, Zoe's mouth dropped open. The fox passed between second base and shortstop, stopping behind the pitcher's mound and Rooster.

She turned back to Penny and said, "Can't they see it?"

Penny shrugged, continuing to watch the spectacle.

Rooster's arms pinwheeled in a comically exaggerated pitch, but before he could release the ball the fox stepped up behind him and grabbed the hem of his shorts with its teeth. It yanked them down to his ankles, exposing Rooster's saggy, stained underwear.

The other boys in the field, including Rooster's older brother, exploded in laughter as Rooster's pitch flew wild and he scrambled to get his shorts back up.

Penny was too shocked to laugh, but Zoe laughed hard enough for both of them.

"Do you think we can get it to follow me home? Maybe I could train it to tie his shoelaces together."

Rooster turned and shook a fist at them, as if they'd somehow caused his shorts to fall down.

The fox was gone.

Chapter 7

The Fox and the Box

Penny and Zoe rounded off their day with an exploration of the school grounds, lunch at the little restaurant next to Sullivan's, and a walk along the Chehalis River. Zoe kept stopping to pluck interesting rocks at the water's edge.

Later, they walked to Zoe's house, where her grandmother had fallen asleep on the couch watching her favorite afternoon soap operas. They tiptoed through the small house to Zoe's room, where she showed off her rock collection and a full shelf of books, all of which she had read at least once.

"We used to move a lot," she said. "I never got a chance to make many friends, so I read."

Her reading tastes ranged from Nancy Drew, to Harry Potter, to *Dr. Jekyll and Mr. Hyde.* Most were fantasy, everything from *Lord of the Rings* to *Discworld*. There was even a selection of old geology textbooks, and a few dedicated to nothing but gems and crystals. Some of these had library stickers from towns where Zoe had lived at one time or another.

Penny finally thought to check the clock on Zoe's nightstand, and panicked. It was five till five.

"Don't worry, I'll give you a ride back," Zoe said, guiding her out through the back door, into the overgrown backyard—where Penny saw a bicycle so old and ugly, she would have almost rather been late than accept a ride on it. It was bulky, with faded yellow paint, rust spots dusting the frame like freckles, a worn banana seat, and long, curving handlebars that would have looked at home on a motorbike.

Zoe seemed to have read Penny's mind.

"I'll stay off Main Street," she said with an apologetic look.

Zoe pumped the bike's peddles with reckless abandon, shooting blindly across intersections, hopping over curbs; Penny sat behind her, holding on for dear life.

They skidded to a stop in the gravel parking lot behind the bookstore just as Susan stepped from the back door and locked it behind her.

"There you are," she said upon spotting them. "I thought maybe you forgot about me."

"I didn't forget," Penny lied, climbing down from Zoe's bike. She felt depressed as she stepped toward the old Falcon. The best day she'd had in weeks was at an end now, and the thought of spending the rest of the evening alone in her room, or watching TV in the living room, was unbearable.

"Susan, can Zoe stay over tonight?"

Penny was sure Susan would say no, and equally sure that Zoe would be tired of her company by then.

Susan gave them a quick look, seemed to be making up her mind, and said, "Sure, why not. Do you think your grandmother will let you, Zoe?"

"Maybe," Zoe said, but she sounded unsure. "Can I call and let you know?"

"That's fine. Will you need a ride?"

"No," Zoe said quickly. "I know where you live. The big house on Clover Hill. I can ride my bike."

Penny gave Zoe her phone number, which Zoe wrote down on the back of her hand. Then Zoe was off, spraying a rooster tail of dust and gravel as she peddled toward her house.

Susan watched her until she disappeared around a corner a block away, then turned back to Penny. "Isn't that a long way to ride?"

Penny thought so too, but said, "She does ride pretty fast."

They stopped at the little video store at the end of town and rented a movie in anticipation of Penny's first sleepover, then drove home with the windows open in the waning heat, a comfortable wind blowing through the car.

"Well, what do you think kiddo? Gonna survive out here in the sticks?"

Staring out the window at the blurred countryside, Penny thought she saw something pace them, then disappear into the brush—something furry and red, about the size of a dog.

She smiled.

"It's weird, but I think I'll get used to it."

They were home nearly an hour before Zoe called back.

"I'm coming over, but I have to wait for a little bit." She sounded anxious.

"We can pick you up if you want."

"*No*," she said at once. "I can ride. Really, I like riding."

"Okay, sure," Penny said, a little confused by Zoe's

insistence.

"Um, it'll be a bit, but please don't call. Grandma's going to bed." After offering a hurried "Good bye," Zoe hung up.

Is she embarrassed about Susan meeting her grandma?

Is she afraid her grandma won't like me?

They ignored their grumbling stomachs, deciding to save dinner and the movie for when Zoe arrived. They watched television, and the clock hanging over the hallway entrance.

An hour passed, and still Zoe did not show up.

"I'm going to start dinner now," Susan said. "If she isn't here in a half hour, I'm calling."

As much as Penny wanted to respect Zoe's wishes and not disturb her grandmother, she was starting to worry.

"She said it'd be a while," Penny said, but shut up at the look Susan shot her.

A half hour later their dinner of hamburgers and fries was finished, Zoe's resting on a covered hot plate, as Penny had persuaded Susan to wait until they had eaten.

Fifteen minutes later, Susan searched their phone's caller ID and redialed Zoe's number, then frowned and hung up.

"It's busy," she said, "or off the hook."

Penny's nerves could take no more, and when Susan suggested they go for a drive to look for Zoe, she didn't argue. However, they hadn't made it off the front porch, before they saw her in the distance, pedaling up their long driveway.

Penny sighed, and relaxed a little.

"Hi," Zoe said, and frowned when she saw the keys hanging from Susan's hands. "Where are you going?"

"To look for you," Penny said. "We were getting

worried."

"I told you I'd be a while," Zoe said, rolling her eyes. She looked touched just the same.

"We called first," Susan said, and Zoe shot Penny an irritated look that made her blush a little. "The line was busy."

"Yeah, sometimes Grandma leaves it off the hook when she goes to sleep."

Zoe forgot her annoyance when they mentioned her waiting dinner, and once seated she wolfed down her burger and fries. When she'd finished, she put a hand over her mouth and belched, then relaxed back in her seat. "That was excellent, Ms. Taylor. I'm stuffed."

"Hope you have room for popcorn," Penny said, tossing a bag into the microwave.

"Always room for popcorn," Zoe replied, and smiled more widely than Penny had seen her smile all day, as they walked to the living room to start the movie.

"Cool room!"

Penny felt as though she were glowing with pride. "It's okay."

Zoe stashed her clothes in the unused dresser while Penny plopped down on her bed. She was so tired she could barely keep her eyes open, but felt too excited to sleep.

Zoe stood at the little window overlooking the vast property in front of their home. "It's like being in a castle," she said.

A strange yip broke the silence of the night, making Zoe flinch. She strained to see something in the distance outside, then gasped.

"What?" Penny said, rising and crowding in beside her

to see outside.

"I don't believe it," Zoe said, and pointed in the direction of the tall wild grass bordering the driveway.

Penny saw it standing down there, a dark four-legged shape in the pale moonlight, its narrow face pointed in their direction.

"Let's go," Zoe said. "I want a closer look."

"Are you crazy?" Penny asked.

"Oh, come on. It can't be too dangerous," Zoe said. "It could have bitten Rooster's butt off if it wanted too. It only pulled down his tighty-whities."

"I don't know," Penny said. "There's something really weird about it. How come only we can see it?"

Zoe shrugged and stepped away from the window, grabbing Penny's arm and dragging her toward the attic door. "I don't know."

Penny tugged her arm loose and frowned as Zoe turned back to her impatiently. "Come on."

Penny decided it was time to tell her, and simply hope that Zoe didn't decide she was nuts—hope she didn't decide not to be her friend anymore.

"I saw it the other day, out on the hill over there. It talked to me."

Zoe's annoyed expression faded, then turned into gape-mouthed disbelief. For several long moments she just looked at Penny, unblinking. Then, finally, she said, "No it didn't. You're pulling my leg."

Penny sighed, and didn't resist as Zoe renewed her grip on her arm.

"Fine, be quiet though." Penny was reasonably certain Susan wouldn't kick her out if she got in trouble. However, she didn't want to test her patience so soon.

They lowered the sliding stairs to the hallway below,

Penny cringing at the squeal it made. She'd have to grease it if she was going to make a habit of sneaking out. They moved quietly through the house and out onto the porch, closing the door behind them as softly as they could.

The fox stood in the same spot, watching them.

"Come on, let's get closer," Zoe said, urging Penny forward.

"What if it comes for us?" Penny asked, her apprehension growing with their proximity to the strange animal.

"Well," Zoe said. "You're so short, it'll catch you easily. By the time it's finished with you, I'll be back inside."

"You think of everything," Penny said.

The fox chuckled at them, and Penny thought she saw it wink in the moonlight.

Then it was gone.

Before she knew it, they were giving chase, Zoe still clinging to her arm.

It was amazing they made it so far without tripping over the many large rocks, bushes, and stunted trees along the path to the hill. The pace was easy for Zoe, who was much faster than Penny. But even she was panting when they finally came to a stop at the bottom of the gentle incline and turned their eyes upward. The silhouette of a dog-like snout with long, pointed ears hung over the edge of the slope, then disappeared into the grass.

"Hurry," Zoe said, and Penny groaned as she struggled up the trail behind her.

This time she made it to the top.

If they expected something spectacular or even mildly interesting at the peak, they were disappointed. The top of the hill opened on a field like the one below, stretching as far as they could see into the darkness. They dashed forward after the sound of something crashing through the tall wild grass, and found themselves on a well-beaten trail.

They ran on and on, the sounds or silhouette of the fox always just ahead of them, and then all at once, Zoe cried out and stopped.

Penny skidded in the dirt, almost crashing into her. She could hear the sound of rushing water, just as she had the last time she'd approached the hill, yet very close this time, not just a phantom sound carried to her on the wind.

"What did you do that for?" Penny dusted off the legs of her jeans and picked a ladybug out of her bangs.

"Look," Zoe said, and pointed.

Penny followed her finger and saw.

Only a few feet in front of them, the trail ended abruptly. The ground descended sharply into a small, tree-choked canyon. The highest boughs of the thick grove before them were level with the high ground they stood on.

The girls stood still for a few moments, peering into the darkness below. Then Zoe grabbed Penny's arm.

"Let's go."

"Yeah," Penny said, turning back the way they had come.

Zoe stopped her. "No...down there."

"I don't know about that," Penny said, looking apprehensive.

Zoe had already moved forward though, as eager to continue the adventure as Penny was to turn back.

"Don't give up now, young ladies." Penny recognized the voice that came from the grove below as the voice of the fox. "You've almost caught me."

Zoe gasped and her mouth fell open.

Without another thought, Penny started down the

drop.

"Hey, wait!" Zoe followed her.

They half climbed, half slid down the steep trail for a minute before they reached the bottom, and pushing through a curtain of hanging willow whips, stepped into a large grove.

For some reason, where the night outside the grove was very dark, the night inside was much brighter, as if it had captured the moonlight and amplified it. There was a ring of stones, a fire pit, covered with dust and surrounded by weeds. The stones on the inside of the ring were burned dark from fires long past, but the center bore no evidence of recent use. The fire pit was surrounded by larger stones, boulders almost, like primitive chairs set around a campfire. Beyond, a wide creek babbled, its surface sparkling and clear. A solid granite wall rose into the darkness on the creek's far side.

The place had a comfortable feel to it: secluded, secret, but welcoming. Someone had used it once, though not recently. Yet Penny couldn't imagine who.

This must be Little Canyon Creek, Penny thought. The very edge of the property she owned.

The most interesting thing about the clearing was the giant, ancient tree standing at the creek's edge. Its large and complicated network of knotted roots snaked across and through the water, as if slowly forming a bridge to the other side. It was easily the strangest tree she'd ever seen up close: its huge trunk twisted, knotted, split, and scarred in places. It looked like it had been struck by lightning at one time, sheared, and a dark-edged wound ran a few feet up the side, ending with a large hole.

There was a scraping sound from the other side of the creek, startling Penny and Zoe into each other's arms.

"What was that?" Zoe asked in a hushed voice.

Penny had no idea, but before she could say so, a swish of red fur emerged from a hole in the solid rock face on the other side of the rushing water. The fox's tail, whipping around as it backed out of a small cave with difficulty.

For several moments the fox struggled, until at last its body and head emerged. Then they saw what had slowed it down. It dragged a small wooden box behind it, its teeth clamped on a leather hand strap. It looked like a pirate's treasure chest with its brass hinges and lock, crossed with leather straps.

When the chest was out, the fox turned to them, its jaw still closed on the handle, and leapt into the water.

"What's it doing?" Penny watched the fox's approach with trepidation, ready to turn and run for it.

"Dunno … playing fetch?"

Halfway across the creek, the fox scrambled up onto the big tree's questing roots, shook the water out of its thick fur, and dragged the chest the rest of the way to the shore. It dropped the chest on the bank and turned to them, panting. It watched them in turn—Zoe first, then, for what seemed like an especially long time, Penny.

"Always the same," it said. Its voice, Penny noticed, had a trace of an accent. British, or maybe Irish? "The new is born from the ruins of the old—the phoenix rises from the ashes, and the adventure continues."

It watched them for a few moments longer, then showed its pointed teeth in what Penny hoped was supposed to be a friendly grin.

"You can call me Ronan," the fox said. "And what may I call you?"

"I'm Penny," Penny said, and when Zoe didn't respond, Penny nudged her.

"Zoe," her friend whispered.

Ronan nodded. "I think you two will do well."

Then it leapt from the stony shore, nimbly springing off the bridge of roots, and vanished back into its cave.

Penny and Zoe tried fruitlessly to open the chest for several minutes, but could not. A sturdy brass lock and a pair of wide hinges secured the lid, and as much as they wanted to see inside, they didn't quite dare to break it. The chest was old, battered, but beautiful. A carving that seemed to be half- bird, half-flame, decorated the top.

"Too bad he forgot to leave the key," Zoe said, disgusted as she set the chest down on the big rock between them.

Penny poked it with a finger and said, "Open sesame."

Nothing happened.

"You didn't really expect that to work, did you?" Zoe asked, and laughed.

Penny shrugged, and yawned. She was surprised she could be tired after all the interesting things that had happened that night, and the mystery of the chest waiting to be solved. It was quite late though. The moon had moved further across the sky, and the grove was growing darker. She wondered if she'd be able to talk Zoe into going back to the house, then her friend yawned too.

"Can you stay for a while tomorrow?" Penny had considered bringing the chest back to her room, so they could spend more time working on opening it, but knew, somehow, that it was a bad idea. The chest was supposed to stay in the hollow.

"Sure," Zoe said. "I left a note for Grandma, told her I'd be going out for the day."

Something about that statement struck Penny as odd, but she let it pass for the moment.

"Good, we can come back tomorrow and try to open it again."

"Try to stop me," Zoe said, sounding excited.

Zoe yawned again, Penny placed the chest inside the abandoned fire ring, covering it with a handful of fallen leaves, and they headed back up the trail, toward home.

They snuck back into the house, up the stairs, and Penny cringed as the steps into her attic room slid down with a slight metallic scraping. They climbed, pulled the steps up behind them, and pulled the door closed behind it. They made it back without Susan catching them, and Penny breathed a little easier.

Exhausted from the long hike back, they dropped into their beds and slept almost immediately.

Penny puzzled over the mysterious chest in her sleep, and Ronan's words echoed in her head.

The phoenix rises from the ashes, and the adventure continues …

Chapter 8

Accidental Magic

Zoe did not get to stay long the next morning. Halfway through breakfast, her grandmother called.

"I gotta go home," she said, sounding worried and angry.

"What's wrong?" Susan downed the last of her coffee and ruffled Penny's hair on her way through the kitchen.

Zoe looked at her lap, a spill of hair falling over her face, and muttered something about *chores*.

"I'm heading to town. We'll stick your bike in the trunk and I'll give you a lift."

Zoe nodded and rose to follow Susan, and Penny saw her face had flushed with embarrassment.

"You coming back?"

"I'll try," Zoe said, and left it at that.

"You can come to town if you want," Susan said. "I can be a few minutes late."

"Naw, I'll stick around today."

"Okay," Susan said. "I only work half days on Saturday, so I'll see you after lunch."

A few minutes later Susan and Zoe were speeding away down the gravel driveway and out of sight.

They'd planned on heading out to the grove after eating, but Penny decided to wait until she'd heard back from Zoe. She watched a few hours of Saturday morning cartoons, but didn't enjoy them. She started reading the book Susan had given her, but couldn't stay interested. The image of that chest, hidden in the ashes and leaves of the fire pit, kept popping into her head, and she grew more restless by the minute. Torn between wanting to get back to that interesting new mystery, and wanting to wait for Zoe so they could work on it together.

They had discovered it together after all. Penny would never have had the nerve to follow Ronan the night before if Zoe hadn't been there to drag her along.

Finally, after finishing a lunch of tuna fish sandwiches and potato chips, Penny decided to call and see if Zoe was coming back.

Penny waited through several rings and was about to hang up when someone, Zoe's grandmother Penny guessed, barked "What?" into her ear.

"Is Zoe there?"

A pause filled with the sound of heavy, wheezing breathing, then, "She's busy."

Before Penny could ask when Zoe wouldn't be busy, the old woman hung up, leaving her in a shocked silence.

Penny waited for a little while longer, but Zoe didn't call back. Finally, Penny set off on her own, walking through the hot, overcast day, toward the grove.

She followed the path she remembered from the day she first saw Ronan, keeping a close watch around her every step of the way for the strange animal. However, Ronan did not show himself. Before long, Penny found herself on the upward slope, gripping the same stunted trees and dry shrubs as before to keep from slipping. At the top, she continued along the path through the wilted wild grass toward a lush green patch in the distance. The top boughs of the grove.

A few minutes later she stood at the edge of the narrow canyon, and gasped as she peered down. From her vantage point, there was no discernible trail down the sheer and stony drop.

How had they gotten down there, and in the dark?

Penny dropped to her knees for a better look down the canyon wall, and saw fresh scuff marks in the dirt. Running her fingers over them, she found a narrow ledge of stone. Craning her neck to look past it, she saw more below.

"This is it," she said, standing up. She took a deep breath, put one cautious foot forward, and stepped down onto the ledge. Then she looked down again, and gasped in surprise. From her new, slightly altered perspective, the way down was perfectly clear. It was as if there had been a blind spot hiding the downward trail, and now that she could see it, it did not seem as far down, or as steep. It looked easy, in fact.

The climb down *was* easy, and once at the bottom, Penny stepped into the clearing, seeing it in full clarity for the first time.

It looked bigger in the light; a high canopy of lush willow leaves let sunlight through in slanted bars. It was as if someone had braided the willow limbs that should have hung over her head into a living canopy. On the outer ring of the grove, the supple limbs hung almost to the ground, except for where the creek ran. On the other side of the creek stood the vertical wall of granite, a small stone ledge only an inch above the rushing water, and the mouth of Ronan's cave.

The large, lightning-scarred tree stood at the water's edge. Looking up, Penny saw that tree was only a little taller than the others, but its trunk was as thick as any five of the smaller trees put together.

An old wooden sign lay on the ground at the big tree's roots, the frayed rope that once held it suspended from one of the tree's lower limbs had rotted and snapped long before.

Aurora Hollow.

The words held a resonance with Penny, like the house, something almost remembered.

Penny turned to the fire ring and felt a jolt of excitement, remembering why she had come. She cleared away the cover of last season's dead leaves and lifted the chest out, dusting old ashes off the wood and the brass-inlaid image of a fiery bird.

A phoenix.

The phoenix rises from the ashes.

Struck by a sudden idea, Penny set the chest aside and plunged her hands into the center of the fire pit. She dug out handfuls of ash and muck, sifting through it.

Penny smiled and raised her fist high, clutching something that glinted in the slanting bars of sunlight. An old brass key.

She ran to the creek's edge, knelt down, and washed the key off, not surprised to see it was a small phoenix with outstretched wings.

"Yes," Penny said.

Trembling with excitement, she walked back to the fire pit and sat down, putting the chest on her lap. She inserted the key with a shaking hand, turned it, and gave a little squeal when the lock popped open with a loud *click*.

The lid opened with a creak, and she stared inside.

Penny let out a sigh of disappointment...It was full of sticks.

She pulled one out and examined it. One end was splintered and ragged, as if someone had snapped it in half, but the point of a small crystal glinted at the other end. Curious, she searched and pulled out another piece and fit the snapped ends together.

A narrow wooden stick with a clear crystal tip.

"Weird."

She pulled more pieces out, matching them up, and counted four broken sticks. One had a red crystal tip, another green. One of the crystals appeared to be made of some kind of crystalline metal.

She found the fifth lying unbroken atop a leather-bound book and plain brass cup, and pulled it out. A shiver ran up her spine as her hand wrapped around it.

A wand, she thought. *How weird is this?*

The wand resembled a dried twist of root more than

anything crafted. It was very thin and twisted, with a tiny clear crystal tip. Penny thought it looked a lot like one of the big tree's roots. The wood was smooth, slightly gray with age, the tip around the crystal point scorched.

She held it up to the light, turning it in her hand until it fit comfortably.

Still feeling a little let down, she dropped the broken wand pieces back into the chest and set it aside.

"So this was the big mystery," she said, and jumped as a small yip sounded from the other side of the creek.

Ronan stood inside the mouth of the cave, all but his pointed face lost to the darkness within.

"Is this it?" She waited for Ronan to respond, but he said nothing, only watched her.

"What now?" She looked from Ronan to the wand, feeling suddenly very stupid. "Do you turn into a prince now, or something?"

Penny gave the wand a little wave and pointed it at Ronan, expecting nothing to happen.

She felt a spark between her hand and the wood of the wand, saw the crystal tip flash briefly, and a rush of wind blew from the wand tip, stirring dust from the ground, rippling the lazy water at the creek's edge, and blowing Ronan's fur back from its head.

Shocked speechless, Penny only stared at Ronan as he stepped forward, blinking in the wind.

"Very good, young lady. I knew you'd figure it out," Ronan said. "But I'll thank you not to point that at me."

Penny jerked her arm down, pointing the wand at the ground, and the wind died.

For several long seconds, Penny tried to speak, but the words seemed to trip over her tongue. Her jaw worked, her mouth opened and closed, but no sound came out.

"You look like a fish when you do that," Ronan said with a dry little chuckle. It stepped from the cave and lay down on the stone ledge by the water.

"What did I just do?" Penny managed at last.

Ronan's eyes opened a little wider and it bared its teeth in a parody of a smile. "I thought that much was perfectly obvious," it said. "Magic."

Penny's knees buckled and she fell heavily onto one of the boulders by the fire pit, dropping the wand into the chest as if it had tried to bite her.

"Probably comes as a bit of a shock, doesn't it?" Ronan yawned. "Well, while you're trying to wrap your mind around it, I'm going to go finish my nap."

Ronan rose, stretched, and stepped back into the mouth of the cave. "Don't normally get out during the day, but I couldn't miss that. Good day, young lady."

Then Ronan was gone and Penny was alone again, staring numb with shock at the wand inside the chest.

"Magic," she whispered.

Her right hand tingled, moved toward the wand, and she forced it to her lap.

"There's no such thing as magic," she whispered, and then, as if to prove it, snatched the wand up again. There was no shock that time, but the tingling in her hand grew stronger. She could not think what to do with it though, so she set it in her lap and reached inside the chest for the book.

The Secrets of The Phoenix Girls decorated the hard leather cover, burned onto it in fancy, looping letters. Below that, a large brass coin with the image of a phoenix inlaid in the leather, and below the coin, burned into the leather like the words above, were two crossed wands.

Penny traced the edge of the embedded phoenix coin with a finger, it felt warm to the touch, and then tried to open the cover. It would not budge.

What now, she thought, frustrated.

She recalled the night before, pointing at the box and saying open sesame, and an idea occurred to her.

She decided, after only a moment's pause, to try it.

What could it hurt?

Penny held the book up in her left hand, grasped the wand in her right, and gave the phoenix coin a poke with the wand's tip.

"Open," she said, feeling more than a little foolish.

The book's cover sprang open immediately, nearly tipping it from her hand.

The top page was blank, as was the next, and the next. Penny rifled through the book, viewing pages at random. They were all blank.

Penny fought the urge to slam the blank book shut and throw it back in the chest with the pile of broken sticks. She sat with it open on her lap, arms folded, bouncing the wand against her arm.

Pop.

Penny screamed and jumped from her seat, spilling the book to the dirt, and spun to see what had made the sudden, loud noise. There was nothing. Then she smelled smoke, felt heat against her leg, and looked down to see her wand's tip issuing a tongue of flame.

Panicking, Penny waved the wand over her head to put out the flame, and screamed again as it let out another loud *pop*. The canopy of joined willow limbs over her head shuddered, shaking leaves down around her.

She dropped the wand, deciding for the moment it was safer out of her hand, and kept a wary eye on it as she bent to pick up the book, still open to the first blank page.

Maybe The Phoenix Girls, whoever they were, used disappearing ink...or magic ink.

An idea occurred to her, and she felt stupid for not having thought of it right away. It was so obvious.

Carefully, she picked the wand up. It did not pop again or shoot flames, so she pointed it at the book, and tapped the first blank page.

Instantly, characters appeared on the old, yellowing paper. The language was alien, composed of stick figures that reminded her of Native American petroglyphs and a thousand complex little runes.

As Penny stared at them, they began to twitch and wiggle, dance and rearrange until they settled on the page in lines of perfect English.

Chapter 9

The Principles of Magic

Penny spent the rest of that Saturday in her bedroom, sitting on her bed reading the same two pages of the book over and over again, and on the phone in the living room, trying to reach Zoe. The first few times it just continued to ring until she gave up. After that, she got a busy signal. She had a feeling Zoe's grandma had taken their phone off the hook.

As desperately as she wanted to talk to Zoe, to share her discovery, Penny decided it might be best to give it up for the rest of the day. Whatever Zoe had done to get in trouble, Penny didn't want to make it any worse for her.

She regretted leaving the wand at Aurora Hollow, wanting badly to hold it again, eager to try what she'd read in the old leather-bound book. Overall, she decided she was better off not using it at home until she knew she could do so without burning the house down, or startling Susan with earsplitting bangs.

"Penny, what are you doing up there?" Susan sounded half-irritated, half-concerned. "You've been hiding since I came home."

Penny waited for the sound of her opening trapdoor, ready to hide the book if Susan decided to come up. Her eyes wandered to the new book Zoe had given her. "I'm just reading."

"Is Zoe coming for dinner?"

"No." Penny frowned, irritated that Zoe hadn't tried to call back.

"Well, it'll be ready soon. Come down and set the table for me."

Sighing, Penny stashed the book beneath her pillow and pulled her shoes on to go downstairs.

They watched television after eating, and Penny went to bed early that night. She was exhausted from the day's excursion and her excitement over discovering the magic at her new home. Disappointment that she couldn't share it with her new friend kept rising in her, but she reminded herself that there was always the next day, or the one after that.

All that night she dreamed of phoenixes and foxes, magic books and magic wands. She dreamed of the two pages of *The Secrets of The Phoenix Girls* that were now visible to her.

She woke the next morning with the tall figure of Zoe leaning down over her.

"Good morning, Little Red." Zoe sat on the edge of her bed, chuckling.

Penny groaned. "Susan! Did you have to tell her about that?"

Zoe laughed. "Sorry about yesterday. Grandma grounded me."

"What for?"

Zoe blushed. "She told me I couldn't spend the night, so I snuck out after she went to bed."

"Does she know you're here now?" Penny asked, alarmed.

"Naw," Zoe said. "Don't worry. She's at church. She'll be

gone most of the day."

"But …"

"C'mon," Zoe said. "I wanna go back and see the chest!"

"Oh," Penny said, feeling slightly guilty, "about that."

Penny told Zoe about finding the key, but wasn't sure how to tell her about what happened afterward.

"Well," Zoe said, not at all upset she'd missed the opening. "What's in it?"

Penny hesitated, then reached beneath her pillow and pulled out the old book.

"Wow!" Zoe practically danced in place, then snatched the book from Penny's hand. "Hey, why won't it open?"

Penny sat up in bed, swung her legs over the side and searched for her shoes. "You're going to have to see it to believe it."

They stood in Aurora Hollow a half hour later, gazing down into the open chest, and Zoe looked as disappointed as Penny had felt upon seeing inside it the first time. Then her eye caught the gleam of crystal, and she reached in, plucking out the broken wand with the green crystal tip.

"Colored quartz," she said, and tried to pry it from the wood.

Penny reached in and pulled out the unbroken wand, and decided on the spot to try out what she'd read the night before. She pointed the wand at the piece of broken wood in Zoe's hand, concentrated, and gave the wand an upward jerk.

The broken wand slipped from Zoe's grasp and hovered in the air a few feet above them. Penny was so surprised by her success that she let it drop. It landed on Zoe's head and bounced into the fire pit.

Zoe stared at it, bent to pick it up again, but hesitated as if afraid it might jump out at her. Instead, she turned toward Penny, her eyes going wide at the sight of the wand she held.

"How did you do that?"

Penny did not answer, but held out the book to Zoe, who took it with a look of bewilderment. Penny tapped the phoenix coin on the cover and it sprang open, displaying the same text to her as the day before.

"Wild," Zoe said, and turned the first page. "There's nothing in it."

Penny was only momentarily stymied by this.

"You have to do it then," she said, and handed Zoe the wand.

Zoe accepted it with a look of excitement. "What now?"

"Tap the pages."

Zoe did, and grinned as the alien print appeared to her, then transformed to English. She tapped the second page, and the same thing happened, but the third remained blank. She tapped it again, but still nothing happened.

"It only showed me the first two pages," Penny said. "I think maybe we have to learn them before it shows us more."

Zoe flipped through all the blank pages of the book, her eyes and smile growing wider.

"Is this … is this real?" She turned to Penny, excitement and skepticism pulling her features in contradicting directions. "Are you playing a joke on me?"

"Go on," Penny urged. "Try something."

Zoe scanned instructions on the second page for a minute, then set the book down beside the chest. She pointed the wand at the debris inside the fire pit, concentrating until her face was almost as red as Penny's hair. The tip flashed, and a spark shot from it, erupting into a small ball of fire that winked out in midair. Smoke drifted into her face, and she waved it away, coughing.

"Was that real enough?" Penny asked, smiling.

The Principles of Magic.

Ability.

One must have a degree of natural ability to feel, channel, and control magical energy. No amount of study, theory, or practice will help a person without natural talent to use magic.

Intention.

Clear intention is vital in channeling magical energy for a specific task. Without clear intention of what you expect channeled energy to do, anything could happen. Most accidents and unintended effects happen because the user's intentions were not clear. Know what you want to do before you try to do it.

Focus.

Without proper focus to propel channeled energy, the intended magic will be weak, or may not work at all. Concentrate on your goal.

Imagination.

Imagination is the key to developing new kinds of magic, and expanding uses for known magic.

This book will only open for one with the ability to use magic. Keep it safe, for it holds the secrets and lessons of those who came before you. Study the secrets of The Phoenix Girls, practice their lessons, and when you are ready, the book will give you more.

Learn and grow, and when the time comes that you have learned all the book has to teach, you will become the teachers.

You are The Phoenix Girls.

Penny practiced while Zoe read the principles of magic written out on the first page of the old book again, first picking up and moving a fist-sized rock with the wand, then making it fly in circles over their heads around the hollow.

"It's like a school textbook." Zoe said, setting the book down and glaring at it, as though it were being intentionally boring.

Distracted, Penny turned to Zoe and lost control of the flying rock, sending it shooting through the upper boughs and startling birds into flight.

"Yeah, but not at first. I think it changed for us because that's how we're used to learning."

"How would it know that? It's a book!" Zoe turned away from the open book, arms crossed stubbornly over her chest—but snatched it up a few seconds later, unable to resist the temptation to reread it.

Penny pointed the wand at the inside of the fire pit, her pale face flushing as she concentrated. The wand tip flashed, and a bright spark shot into the center of the stone ring, erupting into tall, bright flames. Without proper fuel to sustain the fire, it guttered and died in only a few seconds. "Just know what you want to do, then point, and concentrate."

Zoe turned to the second page and scanned it. "I want to try something."

Penny handed the wand over and stood back.

"Throw something at me," Zoe said.

Penny thought she knew what Zoe was going to try, but hesitated. "Are you sure?"

"Yep. If it doesn't work, I'll jump out of the way. Just make it something small."

Penny pried a small stone from the dirt. She still didn't

think it was a good idea, but threw it anyway, aiming to the right of Zoe instead of at her.

Zoe whipped the wand up, pointing it straight out in front of her, her eyes narrowed in concentration. A foot away from her, the stone stopped abruptly and bounced back toward Penny, landing at her feet.

Zoe gave a little shout of triumph. "It worked! Here, you try it."

She ran forward and pressed the wand into Penny's hand, then ran to the creek's edge, plucking a small rock from the water.

"Ready?"

"No," Penny said, but raised the wand anyway.

Zoe grinned, made a show of winding for a pitch, and threw it.

Penny tried to concentrate on making a shield to block it, but her brain froze as she saw it whizzing toward her, and all that happened was that the wand gave a feeble little *hoot*. She jumped out of the way at the last second, and the rock just missed hitting her.

"Oh! I'm sorry," Zoe said, running forward.

"It's okay," Penny said, though her heart was beating hard at the near miss. "Maybe we should practice that one with something softer next time."

They took turns with the wand for the next three hours. While their efforts yielded unpredictable, often nearly disastrous results, they at least had a handle on the few spells—if spells are what they really were—that the book had to offer.

There were no 'eyes of newts' or 'bat wings' involved, no magic words or incantations. Penny didn't think these were spells, only crude manifestations of will. Potions and fancy words would come later, if at all, she guessed.

Why guess when we can check?

"Zoe, come here," Penny said, taking a seat on a boulder by the dead fire pit and picking up the book again. It had closed itself while they practiced, and Penny didn't need to try the cover to know it wouldn't open.

Zoe, who had been using the wand like a leaf blower, sending the cover of dead and rotting leaves off the ground of the hollow and under the curtain of low-hanging willow limbs, turned to Penny. When her concentration broke, the wind blowing from the wand tip died.

"What?" she asked, trotting to Penny's side.

"Let's see if there's anything new."

Zoe brightened at the suggestion, and tapped the Phoenix coin inlaid in the leather cover. The book's cover sprang open, and Penny thumbed the first few pages over to the first blank page.

Zoe tapped it without hesitation, and her grin widened. She pressed the wand into Penny's waiting hand and Penny tapped the page.

Print spread across the page, not the weird pictures and runes, but neat and crisp handwritten English. She tapped the next page, and more text appeared across the top of the page. Beneath the text several illustrations appeared. They looked to Penny like pictures in an instruction manual. She flipped the page and tapped the next.

"Nothing on this one," she said, a little disappointed, and passed the wand back to Zoe so she could read the second new page.

Zoe tapped it with the wand tip and read, taking several long moments to digest it. Her anticipatory grin wilted, became a frown. Finally, she groaned and handed the book back to Penny.

Penny scanned the first new page, skimming over what appeared to be a few more spells, and an illustration of a cup like the one they found with the book. Finding nothing there to frown about, she moved to the second page.

She read it three times, very slowly, before looking up from the page with a sinking feeling of disappointment.

"Magic circle," she said. "We have to make a magic circle before it'll show us more."

Scanning back to the illustration of the cup, rereading the instructions below it, she saw that the book told them how to make the magic circle. It sounded easy, and everything they needed was here, except for one thing.

The one thing they needed to move forward in their learning, neither girl knew how to find.

The book said there must be at least three to start the magic circle, and they were only two.

They needed to find someone like them, someone who had a talent for magic.

They needed another friend.

Questions.

The girls had a hundred of them.

Penny and Zoe sat across from each other on the ground next to the dead fire pit, a reluctant Ronan resting on his haunches between them.

He turned his face from one to the other, then back again, and they fired questions without pause, determined to get them all out.

"This feels like an ambush," he'd said, and he had been right.

"How long have you been here?" Penny asked.

"How long have The Phoenix Girls been here?" Zoe fired her question a second later, before Ronan had a chance to even consider Penny's.

"Why doesn't everyone know about this place?" Penny asked, crossing her arms and leaning closer to Ronan with an inquisitorial eyebrow arched.

For the past few days Penny and Zoe had spent every possible minute at Aurora Hollow, and whenever Ronan came out to watch them practice, the questions began. At first they were hesitant, almost shy. But the more Ronan didn't answer, the bolder they became, until finally Ronan emerged from the solitude of his cave one morning to find them simply standing on the other side of the creek, waiting for him. The wand and book were still locked in their chest.

"Why are we the only ones who can see you?" Zoe asked.

"Enough questions," Ronan growled, apparently pushed to the edge of his patience. "You two should be practicing."

Penny rolled her eyes skyward.

"Why should we be practicing?" Zoe countered, ignoring the renewed growls rumbling up from Ronan's throat. "Why is it so important to you anyway?"

Ronan's feeble attempt at intimidation ceased and he turned to face Zoe again.

So did Penny. That was a question, she thought, feeling a little stupid, which should have occurred to her.

"Yeah," Penny said, catching the thread of Zoe's new enquiry. "Why is it so important?"

Ronan shook his head in frustration. "This is precisely why some animals eat their young."

Zoe giggled.

Penny rolled her eyes again.

"Can you at least answer one of our questions today?" Penny asked, despising the whining tone of her question but unable to help it. "Then we'll practice."

Ronan considered them again in turn, then mimicked Penny by lifting his snout to the sky and rolling his eyes. "If you insist … I will answer *two* of your questions today."

Penny and Zoe sat up straighter, irritation turned into anticipation. They both leaned in a little closer to Ronan.

Penny's excitement grew stronger as seconds passed with Ronan only staring into the distance, silent and still.

Then he turned to Zoe.

"Pick me up."

Zoe seemed startled by the request. They were still a little intimidated by him, such a strange and unlikely creature roaming around boring old Dogwood, but after only a moment's hesitation, she rose to her feet then bent to pick him up. She wrapped her arms around his middle gingerly, as if afraid he'd turn on her and bite, and when she rose again he lay in the cradle of her arms like a pet.

He looked down at Penny. "Anybody can see me if I want them to, but humans have an unfortunate tendency to shoot at things that walk on four legs."

Ronan closed his eyes, and for a second Penny thought he was going to take a nap right there in Zoe's arms. His outline blurred, his body became translucent, and he fell through Zoe's arms and drifted downward toward the ground like smoke. Then he was solid again and falling toward the ground. He landed gracefully on all fours and sprang into the air again, scrambling up the side of the big tree and stopping on his usual high perch.

"I am proficient at escaping your kind, but it's easier just to avoid their notice."

Zoe was still staring into her empty arms in surprise. "That was seriously cool!"

"The reason you can see me even when they can't is because you are different. You may find you see a lot of things the others don't."

"How did you do that?" Penny nearly shouted.

Ronan ignored this latest question.

"The reason only you two know about this place is because the others who came here before you knew how important it was that it be kept secret. People like you are gifted, but they can still die at the hands of a mob."

Penny had no reply for that. The morning's light mood had departed. She met Zoe's eyes and saw the new, serious mood had taken her too.

"If other people learn about Aurora Hollow and The Phoenix Girls, eventually the wrong people will. You would no longer be safe. This place would no longer be safe, and too much depends on …"

Here his speech broke off. He seemed to have thought better of the direction he was leading them.

"What?" Penny and Zoe asked in unison.

Ronan shook his head, and a glimmer of his normal good humor seemed to have returned. "I've answered two questions, just as promised. Now get back to work before I change my mind about eating you."

Part 2

The Red Magician

Chapter 10

Dogwood School

There was only one school in Dogwood, the one at the end of downtown beside the riverside park, where Main Street turned sharply to the left before winding its way toward the coast. Penny's house was less than a mile from the school, so she rode the new bike Susan bought her instead of taking the bus.

The old school building housed kindergarten through high school, every student in Dogwood, which was still fewer than Penny's grade alone back in the city.

The school bus passed her as she neared town, and she saw Rooster's stupid, round face pressed against a window. He made a rude hand gesture and ran his tongue out at her. A few others sitting around him had turned to face her as well, flashing grins that made Penny even more nervous about her first day at her new school. She recognized a few of the faces from the park, the day she'd met Zoe.

She slowed and turned into the school parking lot a few minutes later, suddenly feeling only half her already diminutive size. All those new faces, many of them turning to regard her, the stranger in their town, were a little frightening.

Ignoring the strange, gawking stares, Penny searched for one of two things, the bike rack, or Zoe. She found them both at once as Zoe coasted past an emptying bus, ignoring the pointing fingers and laughter as she passed Rooster and his friends. Her bike looked very poor parked between a new mountain bike and a ten-speed. The owner of the mountain bike, a girl about their age Penny thought, regarded Zoe's antique-looking bike with distaste before clicking the lock on her chained wheel and walking away.

"Zoe," Penny called as she coasted in behind her and slid off the seat, which even adjusted down all the way was a little too high for her.

Zoe turned, looking a little alarmed, but relaxed into a smile when she saw Penny. "Hey Little …" she started, but must have seen the dismay that Penny felt. "Hey Penny!"

Penny had seen Zoe only in passing for the past week, as Susan and Zoe's grandma, a sour woman with thin and tightly curled gray hair, deep-set wrinkles, and a perpetual grimace, took them on their separate courses around town and out of it to Centralia, the nearest small city. These back to school shopping trips had left Penny feeling anxious and a little sick to her stomach.

Penny parked her bike, and they compared schedules. She was disappointed that they only had two of the same classes together, the one before lunch, and the second to last of the day.

"Susan said I could go to the shop for lunch," Penny said as they wound their way through the thickening crowd streaming through the school building's front door. "Wanna come?"

"Yeah," Zoe said, with some excitement.

Zoe could, and had, browsed the bookshelves in Susan's store for hours. More than once Penny had had to drag her out the door.

"I'd rather eat road kill than the school lunch," Zoe said, and Penny's already queasy stomach seemed to roll over.

The first half of that first day was an exercise in self-control for Penny. The overly curious looks, the talking behind hands, and the pointing fingers were uncomfortable enough, but she could handle them. The giggles from the town girls when she passed them in the halls and the occasional mockingly shouted "Hi *Little Red*" from Rooster and his friends turned a merely uncomfortable experience into an excruciating one.

She didn't have to wonder how that now hated nickname had spread so far so quickly, since only three people in Dogwood had known it, and the only one of the three who didn't like her was a teacher at the school.

Her third period, math with Miss Riggs, was the worst of the morning, and her fourth, English with Mr. Cole, who looked a bit like a scarecrow but seemed very nice, was the easiest because Zoe sat next to her.

Penny's hopes of outrunning that old nickname had vanished by lunchtime, as the previously silent mockery became a cappella chorus of "Hi *Little Red*" whenever she passed an unfriendly group. The taunts followed her through the halls, then outside, where they were able to escape to Susan's shop.

They arrived at Sullivan's in moody silence, and Penny was not forthcoming when Susan asked how her first day at school was going. She grunted, shrugged, and mumbled something around a mouthful of glazed doughnut.

"It's a small town," Susan said, as if that explained it. "They don't get many new faces here is all. They'll warm up to you."

Penny's eyes found Zoe, who had escaped the inquisition by ducking into the nonfiction aisle to browse, and was not encouraged. Zoe already had a few months on Penny, and most of the kids were just as indifferent or outright nasty to her.

Maybe they were slow warmers.

It didn't occur to Penny until halfway through the last class of the day that the way things were going, she wouldn't make any new friends, and without at least one new friend, The Phoenix Girls were just words in an old book.

After school they walked to Zoe's house, and Penny endured several uncomfortable minutes in her grandmother's company. Then they rode toward Penny's house, and Zoe mentioned The Phoenix Girls for the first time that day.

"I don't think we'll find another friend for the circle."

Penny made no comment, and Zoe said no more on the subject.

They peddled through the tall green blades and pushed their bikes up the hill to the higher, wilder field, then laid them down in the high grass before the drop into the hollow.

They practiced the spells they already knew, giving the old tricks new twists out of boredom. Penny discovering, while conjuring a wind, one of the first tricks she had mastered, that she could heat or cool it at will. She made a warm wind spin and spiral around the hollow like a mini-tornado.

Zoe practiced directing her shield, making it move farther away from her, closer to her, or directing it over her head like an invisible umbrella.

The atmosphere of oppressive glumness departed when Zoe chased Penny around the fire pit, giving her little static shock zaps with the wand. Their moods lifted even further when they heard Ronan, who had snuck out of his cave and perched himself on a high limb of the strange tree to watch them, laughing heartily in his weird accent.

"Had a tough day at school, did'ja ladies?" Ronan asked

when his laughter had subsided.

This stunned them into silence for a moment.

"Yeah," Penny said. "How did you know?"

"I have my sources," Ronan said, and offered his toothy grin. "Don't worry. Things'll turn around. They always do."

"I don't think so," Zoe said, her mood turning dour again. "The kids here are awful."

Ronan cocked his head to the side and hunched his front shoulders in an almost comic imitation of a shrug. "All kids are awful," he said.

"Hey," Penny said, taking offense. "I'm nice!"

Ronan gave her a look, and she could almost read the expression on his furry face.

Who you trying to kid, missy?

Then he broke into that toothy grin again and said, "Just because you're awful doesn't mean you can't be nice. It's a matter of perspective."

"What is that supposed to mean?" Zoe asked.

Ronan shook his head. "Now if I explain it all to you, what is left for you to learn?"

"You're not being very helpful," Penny said, crossing her arms and shooting Ronan an irritated look.

"Of course I am," Ronan said, rising on his high limb and stretching, then scurrying down the tree trunk and leaping across the stream onto the little outcropping of rock in front of his cave. "I'm exceedingly helpful. You're just too busy sulking to recognize it."

Ronan disappeared into his cave then, and when the girls tried to call him out, he did not reappear.

"Fuzzy little pain in the butt," Zoe muttered a few minutes later as they climbed the slope out of the hollow.

Penny did not respond. She was too busy trying to decipher the meaning of Ronan's words.

Just because you're awful doesn't mean you can't be nice. It's a matter of perspective.

Though she couldn't grasp the significance of the comment, she was sure Ronan hadn't just made it in passing.

When Penny went to bed that night, it was with a new determination to stop sulking, as Ronan had put it, and try to find out how her classmates could be awful and nice at the same time.

It's a matter of perspective.

She'd have to change her perspective, she supposed, but still wasn't sure how she was supposed to do that, or even what Ronan meant by it.

The next morning went much the same as the first, the turned heads, giggles, and pointed fingers as she and Zoe chained their bikes up and went inside the school building. After parting ways with Zoe, Penny passed the library on her way to her homeroom, and saw Rooster eyeing a little girl as she walked by with a stack of books in her arms. As she passed him, Rooster reached out and swung a fisted hand upward between her clutching hands, knocking her stack of books flying.

Penny froze in shock and anger, watching as Rooster and a few of his ever-present friends burst into laughter.

The girl's face burned red in embarrassment as she bent down to gather her books and Rooster kicked one away from her reaching hand.

Penny was moving through the library door toward him before she knew she meant to do it, her trembling fists swinging at her sides.

Rooster grinned in surprise and mischief at her approach, but his smile melted into a wide-eyed look of shock as his eyes flicked over her shoulder.

Someone pushed Penny rudely aside.

"Hey!"

The girl who'd shoved her aside ignored her and stalked toward Rooster, a half-dozen friends following in her wake. She stepped up to him without hesitation and shoved him.

"Hey, stop it," Rooster cried, managing to sound like the victim. "C'mon!"

"Make me stop it," she said, and Penny recognized her as the girl who'd given Zoe's bike a distasteful look the morning before. "Come on big man."

She shoved him again, and with a gaggle of her friends backing her up, Rooster and his few friends didn't quite dare to do anything.

"Geez, Katie, I was just having a little fun," Rooster grumbled, and slunk away toward the exit at the other end of the library.

Laughing at Rooster's retreat, Katie's friends began to gather the younger girl's books for her.

Penny's initial shock and anger had turned to happy

surprise as she watched this.

Guess they aren't all jerks, she thought, and stepped forward to help.

"What are you looking at, Little Red?" Katie caught Penny's eye and rose to face her, her eyes narrowing.

Penny stopped short, stung. "I just wanted to help."

Katie apparently thought this unworthy of a reply, and handed the book in her hand to the now smiling young girl.

"Scram, Little Red," one of the others said.

Fighting back the tears that pushed and stung the corners of her eyes, Penny scrammed.

By the end of the first week, the jeering and teasing had mostly subsided, and with a few exceptions, the local kids turned their efforts in other directions.

Penny could deal with that, she supposed. The indifference most of the other students treated her with wasn't what she had hoped for, but it beat the constant teasing. A few of the town kids even started being nice to her, but none made any effort to befriend her.

Katie and her small group of friends treated her with the same contempt as before, yet at least they left her alone.

Rooster and his friends taunted her whenever chance allowed.

By Friday afternoon, Penny and Zoe had fallen into a bearable routine: trudging through their morning classes, lunch at Susan's shop, and spending their afternoon classes looking forward to the few hours they'd spend at the hollow after school.

Late Friday evening, the coals of Penny and Zoe's fire in the hollow had cooled from orange to a dead and powdery gray. However enough of their spent magic lingered to make the still air hum softly. It was a sound too low for Penny or Zoe to hear. Yet the animals that lived near Little Canyon Creek felt it and responded, converging on the spot that had been theirs alone for years, and which had only recently seen people again.

A squirrel leapt from branch to branch in the upper boughs of the willows, catching more air than it normally would have, almost seeming to hover in the open space between branches. A flock of sparrows circled, twittering madly until an owl hooted them away. A long snake cut wild, swirling wakes in the calm water near the shore of the creek.

Predators cavorted alongside their natural prey in the boundaries of Aurora Hollow, their interest in meat temporarily eclipsed by the buzzing residue of magic.

Sometimes Ronan was there too. The other animals recognized him for what he was, but trusted and helped him whenever he asked something of them.

He was there that Friday night, curled up and sleeping in the mouth of his cave.

A discordant buzz drove away the peaceful hum, a sound that set Ronan's teeth on edge and made him whimper in momentary discomfort. His fur began to rise, as if with static.

The other animals scattered in every direction, the owl giving a disconsolate hoot as it abandoned its perch.

A thin glowing line like a thread of violet fire cut the dark—slashing downward from a height of ten feet until it touched the ground. For a few moments the line only buzzed and flickered in the dark. Then two sets of fingers pushed through it, widening it into a crack. The fingers forced themselves into the hollow from behind the widening crack, became hands—one holding something slender and dark—then a pair of cloak-draped arms followed the hands.

Ronan stood, his ears perking up as he turned to face the

crack in reality.

The opening wavered and groaned as a tall man pushed through it; and for only a moment, another place was visible behind him. It could have been a wide cavern or the dungeon of some medieval castle.

Then he was through, the slender black wand in his hand held out before him. He searched around as the rough oval shape with the crackling violet outline contracted, then slammed closed and vanished with a *snap* like a firecracker.

Ronan growled, an uncharacteristic sound coming from him, his teeth now bared in threat rather than humor, and rose, his fur bushing up.

The man whirled on his boots, wand whipping around toward the growling fox, and a bright red flash lit Aurora Hollow like high noon.

The man's spell hit Ronan as he leapt from the mouth of his cave.

With a yelp, Ronan smashed back against the granite wall. His form faded, became a crackling outline in the darkness, and he was gone before he could hit the ground.

The man was still for a moment, watchful, and then turned back to the empty clearing. He muttered, jabbed the slender black object into the air over his head, and a globe of light bloomed from its tip, floating lazily toward the canopy of leaves.

The man lowered his wand, but kept it ready at his side.

For a few minutes he did not move. He scanned the hollow very slowly, taking in every detail.

"Green," he said. He had a faint accent, one that was impossible to place.

He raised his wand again in an almost lazy gesture, and the cracking of wood sounded overhead. A small limb crowded with leaves sailed down to him, as if on gentle wind.

He snagged it from the air and plucked a single leaf. He

held the leaf to his face, sniffed it, and let it flutter to the ground. He tossed the twig toward the fire pit, and while it was still in the air, whipped his wand upward, pointing at it. The wand's tip flared, and a flash of red light touched the twig, enveloping it.

The living wood and fresh green leaves crackled, warped, shriveled, and fell toward the coals of the fire pit. When it landed among the cold coals and half-burned wood, it scattered like ash.

He stalked past the fire ring and stopped at the edge of the hollow, searching the ground as he walked. He used the wand while he searched, moving the tip back and forth over the ground like a dousing rod. Then, suddenly, it dove toward the ground, making the man stagger forward a step.

When he raised the wand again, something followed it up from the ground, pushing dirt and years of accumulated rubbish aside.

The thing followed him as he backed out of the trees, to the edge of the hollow, obeying the direction of his wand like a marionette. He stopped by the fire pit, urging it forward until it wedged between two narrow willows.

It was a door. Old, dirty, set into a snug frame that wedged perfectly between the two trees. Its old brass knob was filthy and tarnished, and undoubtedly frozen in place by years of corrosion.

Smiling, satisfied, the man turned quickly, his wrap of black cloak swirling around him. His red hair stood from his head like flames frozen in mid-dance.

The hand with the wand disappeared beneath his cloak, and reappeared a second later holding a wooden flask. He crouched at the water's edge, uncapped the flask, and dipped it beneath the clear, running water. When it was full, he capped it and stowed it inside his cloak again.

He strode back to the door with his wand drawn,

muttered, and rapped the wood of the filthy door sharply with it.

When he grasped the knob it worked roughly, but it did work. He opened the door. However it did not open onto the density of willows and brush on the other side of it, but, somehow, rather on the lamplit semidarkness of downtown Dogwood.

Glancing once more around Aurora Hollow, he said, "They're back."

He smiled then, turned sharply toward the door, and strode through it.

Boots that had made no sound on the dirt ground of Aurora Hollow clapped loudly on the blacktop on the other side of the door.

He swept it closed behind him, and once again the hollow was empty.

Chapter 11

Tovar The Red

Tonight only in Dogwood Park,
experience the magic of Tovar The Red.
He will amaze you!
Free admission–Showtime 8:00 to 9:00 PM.

Beneath the large, extravagant text of the flier pinned to the telephone pole, one of many it seemed—every pole, notice board, and window in town seemed to have one—was a picture of a man with a narrow, handsome face covered with red stubble, and red hair that stood from his head like flames. There was no magician's top hat in either his hands or on his head, just a simple black cloak draped over his wide shoulders, a simple white shirt tucked into black pants, and black boots with heels that added another few inches to his tall, narrow frame.

In one of his wide-stretched hands he held a plain black wand. In the other, a small oval mirror that reflected the face of a wonderstruck teenage girl.

"We have to see this," Zoe said, yanking the flier from the tack that held it. Then, almost whispering, "I wonder if he's ... you know, for real."

Penny didn't respond. Her eyes followed the face of the red-haired man, Tovar The Red, as the flier moved with Zoe's gesturing hand.

"I mean, if he's real maybe he can help us. I bet he knows stuff. Maybe he can show us…Penny?"

Penny snatched the flier from her hand, still not responding, and held it close to her face.

"Earth to Penny," Zoe said, waving her hand between Penny's nose and the flier.

Penny flinched back, blinking, and looked up at Zoe. She felt numb, stunned and slow.

Zoe's good-natured grin vanished. "What's wrong?"

Penny handed the flier back wordlessly and dug in the front pocket of her jeans for her coin purse. She pulled it out, almost dropped it, and fumbled with the zipper, finally catching hold of it and drawing it back with a metallic rasp. She pulled a photograph out, examined it, and handed it to Zoe.

Zoe regarded the photo, her eyes growing wide. They flicked back to the flier, stopping there for a moment, then back to Penny.

"Who is it?"

For a few seconds Penny's silence held, then she swallowed, as if trying to clear an obstruction in her throat, and croaked two words.

"My father."

They skipped their trip to the rock shop and walked to the park, sitting underneath Zoe's favorite reading tree.

Someone had covered the gazebo in the middle of the park with fliers and large poster boards advertising the free show.

"It looks a lot like him," Zoe conceded, "but..." She seemed unable to finish the thought aloud and only shrugged.

"It looks exactly like him," Penny said. "And he looks like me too."

"But you can't be sure," Zoe said. "Maybe we should show Susan."

"No," Penny said, a little more sharply than she intended. "We can't let Susan see this."

"Why not?"

Penny said nothing for a few moments but seemed to be deep in scheming.

"Why can't Susan see him?"

"Because she hates him," Penny said, turning her green eyes from Zoe's face, regarding the poster at the gazebo.

"Oh."

"We can tell her there's a show in the park, but we can't tell her about him."

Others were filling the park now, migrating toward the gazebo to read the poster. Much speculative chatter filled the day.

"Okay, so we don't tell Susan. She's going to see the posters though."

Penny nodded. "Maybe. But I have to come here tonight. I have to see him."

"Then we will," Zoe said. "If you still think it might be him after watching the show, then we'll find a way to talk to him afterward."

Penny's green eyes found Zoe's brown ones, tears blurring her vision. Her thin-lipped grimace loosened. A small smile had replaced it.

"Thanks," Penny said.

The show started at sunset, and the park was full. It seemed to Penny that every kid in town was there, along with a number of adults.

Penny and Zoe, neither eager to endure more unpleasantness from the local kids, stayed back from the crowd surrounding the gazebo, almost hiding behind Zoe's tree. A girl neither knew, but whom Penny recognized by face as one of the few girls who had been friendly, sat a little ways off from them, alone. She glanced in their direction a few times, as if hoping to be invited over.

Penny returned her wave at one point, forcing a smile, but when they didn't ask her to sit with them, she returned her attention to the empty gazebo, looking disappointed.

Zoe nudged Penny in the side and nodded toward the girl. "We're supposed to try and make new friends," Zoe reminded her.

"Not tonight," Penny said, and faced the lamplit platform of the gazebo, waiting.

The gazebo, Tovar The Red's makeshift stage Penny presumed, appeared newly whitewashed. Tiki torches circled it, waiting to be lit. A thick, dark cloth draped the back half of the gazebo. There were no other visible props, and as the small clock tower at the town square ticked the last few seconds to 8:00 PM, there was no magician.

A small, broken ripple of displeasure rose and spread, until the audience seemed to thrum with discontent.

"This sucks," someone shouted, one of the older boys who had teased Zoe that summer. He rose, tugging at his girlfriend's arm until she followed, casting embarrassed glances back at the crowd.

"Just where do you think you're going?"

The voice boomed across the park. When the audience's eyes moved from the stunned and pale boy standing with his girlfriend's arm clutched loosely in his hand back to the gazebo, they found Tovar The Red standing above them on the raised stage. His grin was wide and good-humored. He held a wand in one outstretched hand, and when he waved it, the dark torches around him blazed to life, casting a dancing light over his stage.

Tovar's wand looked nothing like her wand, Penny noted. Hers was a tapered twist of root, the natural wood grain darkened by age but otherwise unchanged. The crystal at its tip was small, clear as water and with a perfect point at each end, but natural. Tovar's wand was narrow, straight, and had an almost mirror-black sheen. There was a glimmer of reflected light from the polished facets of a small ruby red gem at the tip.

His trick with the tiki torches was neat, a great icebreaker provoking a few *oohs* and *aahs* from the audience—but Penny wasn't convinced yet.

"Come on, son, at least be a gentleman and let the young lady stay for the show." Tovar spoke calmly, softly, but his voice carried over them as if amplified.

He pointed his wand at the girl, and she gave a little shriek of surprise, raising her free hand to regard it. A small bouquet seemed to grow and blossom from the loosely clenched fist her hand made: strange tropical-looking flowers with great drooping bells of orange, purple, a shouting bright red, and an almost neon blue.

The girl laughed in surprise, and applause rippled through the crowd.

"She's a plant," Penny heard a man mutter from

behind, sounding both amused and a little impressed. "It was all planned in advance. Good trick though."

"I am Tovar The Red," the magician said. There was no need to speculate about where his title, *The Red*, came from. His wild red hair waved like flame atop his head in the lazy evening breeze. His eyes, an emerald green as deep as Penny's, glittered in the torchlight. "Welcome to my show!"

Penny had never been to see a live magic show before, but she had watched a few on television—and those were nothing like the one Tovar put on. His stage was too small for the complex kind of props other magicians used, and Penny couldn't see how he would have been able to install a trapdoor in the gazebo floor without having to tear it up first. The floor was clearly visible, clearly unchanged, except for the fresh coat of paint. There was no curtain to escape behind, only the cloth he'd hung as a backdrop from the backside of the rounded ceiling. What props he did use, he seemed to conjure from midair, or to pull from one of what must have been a hundred pockets hidden inside his cloak.

Tovar did not produce a saw and cut anyone in half. However, he did hypnotize several audience members in order to assist him with his tricks.

One of the girls he hypnotized, much to Penny's amusement, was Katie West, the rude girl from the school library. Katie danced a jig (Penny thought it was an Irish River Dance) on the top step of the gazebo. But instead of holding her arms at her side, she'd flapped them briskly up and down like a bird and had levitated off the floor, bobbing in the air for several seconds to wild laughter from the audience.

When she left the stage, her cheeks glowing red with embarrassment in the flickering light of the torches, she spotted Penny in the crowd and shot her a withering look.

The girl who had sprouted a full bouquet of flowers from her clenched fist at the start of the show continued to sprout new flowers throughout. They came from behind her ears, from the pockets of her shorts, from the sleeves of her shirt, and once from her right nostril. Her boyfriend cultivated them with growing amusement, plucking them as they appeared and laying them with the original bouquet, the whole time pestering her to tell him how she was doing it.

She could only shrug, looking equally amused and bewildered.

"And now for a look into the Conjuring Glass," Tovar announced. He pulled a small mirror from beneath his cloak. It was oval, without a handle, and framed in pewter. It fit nicely in the palm of his hand, and he raised it high for the audience to see. "Is anyone here brave enough to peek into the magic glass?"

All through the gathered crowd hands shot up and voices called out eager willingness. Penny's was among them, and after a nudge from Penny, Zoe's hand went up too.

He startled two girls Penny's age—the one who had sat near them earlier and one Penny recognized from her English class—into near hysterics when he invited them onstage and handed them each a mirror, instructing the girls to look into them.

They looked, frozen in near identical expressions of shock, and shouted in alarm. Instead of seeing their own faces in their mirrors, they saw the face of the other looking back.

The illusion (*but was it really an illusion,* Penny wondered) had only lasted a few seconds, and the girls left the stage laughing and clutching the mirrors in their hands, which Tovar insisted they keep as gifts.

He'd repeated the mirror trick a half-dozen times, choosing his volunteers from a forest of raised hands. He matched Katie with one of her friends, then Rooster and his older brother. Rooster had seemed impressed—until his brother muttered something about cheesy tricks and dropped his own mirror in the grass while walking away from the stage. Finally, he called on Penny and Zoe.

Penny had watched Tovar closely throughout the show, but he had given her and Zoe no more than a passing glance until they stood onstage to either side of him.

"Young lady," he said, bowing slightly as he passed the first mirror to Zoe. His movements were sharp and twitchy, his manners forced and curt; Penny thought that despite his profession, he didn't like kids much.

Then he turned to Penny and froze for the barest second, his green eyes going wide, before handing Penny an identical mirror.

"Look into each other's eyes," he instructed. "Clear your minds, then when I tell you, look into the mirrors."

Tovar faced away from Penny and focused his attention on Zoe, who seemed to be growing more nervous by the second.

Penny fixed her eyes on Zoe's, but could not drive the image of Tovar's startled face from her mind. She seemed exquisitely aware of his presence, and as if sensing this, he stepped back from them, turning away to face the backdrop.

"Now," he whispered.

Penny looked into the mirror cupped in her hands, and

could not stop the startled squeal that rose to her lips.

She had expected to see Zoe's face looking out at her, but that was not what she saw.

Though his back was to her, she was positive he was holding his own mirror, gazing into it while they gazed into theirs, because she was looking through hers at his sharply concentrated face.

The expression on his face was plain. It was a look of shocked recognition.

A moment later he shooed them from the stage and called on two more volunteers. After this final pair he ended the show by telling them he would be back in a few weeks for Harvest Days, and that he hoped to see them all there.

Penny was on her feet before he'd finished his final pitch, moving toward the stage again.

"Penny, wait up."

She could hear Zoe behind her, diving through breaks in the dispersing crowd, but did not slow for her.

While Tovar The Red gathered his few remaining props, stowing them into the well-hidden pockets of his cloak, his eyes met Penny's again.

"Penny!" Not Zoe's voice this time, Penny knew that, but didn't turn to see who it was. She was only feet away from the gazebo, and breaking through the last of the milling crowd.

Her fast walk became a jog.

Tovar grinned, pulled his black wand from inside his cloak. Penny stopped, shocked by the certainty that he was going to attack her with it.

Instead, he pointed it at the floor between his feet, and a thick white fog wafted up from between the cracks in the white boards. The fog filled the gazebo within seconds, completely covering him.

"Wait!" Penny started up the steps, ignoring the looks from the thinning crowd, and felt a hand on her shoulder, clamping down hard enough to hurt, stopping her in her tracks.

The fog thinned, faded, disappeared, and Tovar was nowhere in evidence.

Penny shouted in frustration and turned, shrugging the hand from her shoulder.

Susan stood behind her, and the look on her face stole Penny's anger.

Fear?

Chapter 12

Vanishing Act

Penny rode home alone that night; Zoe's grandma was in her usual foul mood and wouldn't let her spend the night. She replayed the scene in the park after Tovar had vanished, and in the dark interior of Susan's store. After sending Zoe home, Susan had told her some very startling things. Penny was glad Zoe wasn't there to hear them. They were revelations she had to consider on her own before she shared them with anyone, even her best friend.

"I know what you're thinking, Penny." Susan held up her hand to stop Penny's denial before she could voice it. "I don't know who he is, not for sure anyway, but I know who you think he is."

Susan turned away then, looking through her shop window at the now empty town park.

She's watching for him, Penny thought. *She's afraid he'll come back.*

When Susan seemed satisfied that no one was watching,

she turned back to Penny. "He's not the first Red Magician to come here. I think there's a family of them, but it has been a long time. They used to come to town with the carnival during Harvest Days every year, and usually left with it. The last time one decided to stay … it didn't turn out well."

"What do you mean?" Penny could sense the conversation hovering somewhere near the heart of the mystery she wanted badly to solve.

Her mystery.

"He's not your father," Susan said, "and even if he was I'd tell you to stay away from him."

Penny felt her face blush red in fresh anger. "What's so wrong with me wanting to find my dad? Mom wouldn't ever talk about him, and I guess you're in her corner! What did he do that was so bad?"

Susan regarded her for a moment, her face a picture of indecision. Her eyes flicked to Zoe, who sat huddled in the furthest chair from Penny and Susan, her eyes fixed on the hands folded in her lap.

When her eyes found Penny again, the indecision was gone, replaced with a grim and hard resolve.

"Zoe, are you coming over tonight?" She asked this without taking her eyes from Penny. She no longer looked angry, only tired.

"No," Zoe said, her voice no more than a whisper. She sounded as if she would rather be anywhere in the world at that moment. "Grandma wants me home for chores."

"You better get home then," Susan said. Then she did look at Zoe, and her expression was kinder, less forbidding. It was the Susan they both knew and loved, not the angry stranger who dragged them inside after Tovar The Red's show. "You're welcome to come over tomorrow, if it's okay with your grandma."

As always, Susan's face darkened a little at the mention of

Zoe's grandma. They were both town women, and Susan knew her well enough to dislike her even though she never spoke a single word against her in either Penny or Zoe's presence.

Zoe relaxed a little and rose from her seat. "Okay. Goodbye."

A few seconds later she was out the door and sprinting down the emptying sidewalk for her home.

When Susan faced Penny again, the resolve on her face was a little frightening. Penny steeled herself for the worst. She'd asked, screamed actually, to hear this, so she would—however bad it turned out to be.

"You were born a month premature. You weighed just under four pounds when I found you. I was sure you were dead. Seeing you like that, on the ground next to your mother, very tiny and not moving, it was the worst moment of my life. I thought you were dead. I thought you were both dead."

A few tears leaked unnoticed from Susan's eyes and fell into her lap.

"What …" Penny's mouth was dry, and she was unable to finish her question. She knew she'd been born prematurely, but always assumed her entrance into the world had been otherwise uneventful. She swallowed, cleared her throat. "What happened?"

"We don't know … not all of it anyway. Diane was out, with *him*." There was real venom in the last word, and Penny didn't need to ask who she meant by *him*.

"Di," Susan smiled briefly, "that's what we called your mom. Never Diana, always Di, and your aunt Nancy had a fight that day, and Di ran off with him. Nancy and her friend Tracy went looking for them …"

"What?" Penny had nearly shouted, and Susan flinched away from her. "I have an aunt?"

Susan regarded her in silence for a moment, then nodded.

"She never told you?"

"No," Penny said, and was unable to keep her resentment to herself. "She never told me anything. I didn't even know who you were until the director at the group home told me you were coming to get me."

Susan nodded. "I guess she just wanted to forget about everything that happened before you came along. A lot of bad stuff happened that night, and then there was you." Susan smiled, tears still shining in her eyes, and Penny loved her for it.

"Nancy was your mother's twin sister, identical in every way but temperament." She smiled again. "Di was very easygoing, very devil-may-care. Nancy was sweet but hot-tempered."

In a much calmer voice, all her anger was gone now, extinguished by the love in Susan's smile, Penny said, "What happened?"

"There was an accident. That old red Mustang she loved so much was in flames, and I found her," she looked up for a second to regard Penny, "and you. She went into labor on the side of the road. She was unconscious when we found her, and you weren't moving at all. Jan, another of our old friends, was with me so she drove you to the hospital in my car."

"That old Falcon?" Penny asked.

Susan chuckled. "No, back then I drove an old VW Minibus. Jan took you to the hospital. I didn't think you'd live, but you were stronger than you looked. I stayed with Di until help arrived. Nancy and Tracy were the first, and by the time they got there your mom was on her feet again."

Penny breathed a little sigh of relief. It was silly; she knew her mom had survived, but didn't like to think about her being hurt.

"Nancy and Tracy both left town a few days later. I don't where they are now, I haven't seen them since they left. I don't know about Tracy, but I think Nancy went looking for your father."

Penny sat in stunned silence for a moment, understanding what Susan was about to say next, but not wanting to believe it.

"He was with her that night, and after the accident …" Susan shrugged. "Like I said, we don't know everything that happened, Di couldn't remember the accident, but your father never came back to find out what happened to you, or to her."

"But you know it's not...," Penny gestured vaguely toward the empty park where Tovar The Red had entertained that night.

"It's not," Susan said.

"How do you know?"

"Because he knows if he ever showed his face around here again, I'd kill him for abandoning you and Di."

Penny didn't know what to say to that, and the look on Susan's face was enough to convince her she might do it.

"What's his name?"

Susan shook her head. "That's enough for one night, kiddo, let's get home. We'll stick your bike in the trunk and you can ride with me."

"No, I'm okay," Penny lied, trying to hide her frustration. "I'll ride my bike home."

Penny didn't think Susan would let her, but after a moment she nodded her head.

"Fine, you get going and I'll catch up to you."

The ride home seemed to go very quickly, or maybe Penny just had too much on her mind to pay attention to the time, and Susan passed her in the old Falcon just before the turn on to Clover Hill.

Though she was dead tired by the time she'd changed into her pajamas and lain down in her bed, it was a long time before Penny slept. When she finally did, her troubled thoughts and endless questions followed her into the land of dreams.

Penny awoke to shouting from below and opened her eyes on bright sunlight slanting down through her parted curtains. Glancing at her alarm clock, she saw it was almost noon.

"Penny, get up! You have a visitor."

"I'm up," Penny shouted. "Give me a minute!"

She rolled out of bed, rubbing the sleep from her eyes, and reached for the clothes lying in a heap at the foot of her bed.

Before she could start to change though, she saw the mirror on her nightstand. She remembered the startled face of Tovar The Red staring up through it, and shivered.

Penny opened the top drawer of her nightstand, put the mirror inside, and after a moment's hesitation, swept a stack of books over it before closing the drawer.

Penny let down the attic door, the ladder sliding smoothly down to the hallway below, and climbed down. She ran down the steps to the hallway, eager to get Zoe away from Susan, to go to the hollow. She wasn't ready to share Susan's story from the night before with Zoe yet, but she wanted her company badly.

Instead of Zoe, she found a man in a khaki uniform, tin star badge, and white Stetson waiting just inside the open front door.

His thumbs hooked into his belt, the right only inches away from his holstered gun. He was speaking with Susan, his expression serious and his bushy white eyebrows drawn together.

Susan looked more than worried; she looked terrified.

Then they saw her coming to a stop halfway down the stairs, and Susan composed herself, drawing a neutral expression over her real one.

Penny had seen the sheriff around town, cruising in his jeep or walking down Main Street, but had never talked to him before. He turned to her, and his grim expression vanished, replaced by a sunny grin full of large white teeth. The name embroidered on his khaki chest was *Price*.

She wondered if he was related to Rooster and his dad. In a town this small, having the same last name, he just about had to be.

"Young Miss Sinclair," he said, sweeping his Stetson off and stepping forward to take her hand. His thin white hair was short as peach fuzz, and the scalp below so deeply tanned it looked like leather.

He took her hand and gave it a single, companionable squeeze.

"What's wrong, sir?" Penny had never been in trouble before, but the sudden appearance of the sheriff...*here to see me?*...made her nervous.

The wattage of his smile dropped considerably, and his expression became businesslike. "You're not in trouble, young lady. I just want to ask you a few questions about Jodi Lewis."

"Who?"

Susan began to pace, passing back and forth behind her. The flashes of her in Penny's peripheral vision, and the clop-clop-clop of her shoes on the hardwood floor were distracting.

The sheriff looked surprised, but hid the expression quickly.

"Yes, you're new here," he said, as if reminding himself.

"Yes," Penny said, feeling the tense silence that had grown and filled the hallway.

"Jodi goes to school with you, she was seen sitting near you and..." he pulled a small, well-thumbed notebook from his breast pocket and fingered through the first few pages. "You and Zoe Parker."

He gave a quick physical description, but Penny didn't need it. Only one person had sat anywhere near them during the show, the girl who had waved at them and smiled expectantly, as if hoping they'd ask her to sit with them. Penny remembered how she had screamed in astonishment when she'd seen another girl's face staring out of the trick mirror at her.

"Yeah, I remember her," Penny said when Sheriff Price had finished giving his description. "What do you want to know about her?"

Susan stopped pacing, standing directly behind Penny, and put her hands on Penny's shoulders, squeezing them.

"Did you see her at all after the show last night? Do you know where she might have gone?"

Penny did not. She'd been too sharply focused on Tovar in the aftermath of the show to notice where anyone else might have wandered.

She shook her head. "Sorry."

Sheriff Price considered her for a moment, his steady dark eyes seeming to probe her, and he nodded. "If you do remember anything, anything at all, please call me. It's very important."

Understanding it might not be wise to ask questions of her own at that point, understanding it might even earn her a scolding from the now stony-faced sheriff, but overcome by her natural curiosity, Penny said, "What did she do?"

Sheriff Price glanced over her shoulder for a moment, as if asking Susan's permission to answer, and then focused on Penny again.

"Well, young lady, Jodi Lewis went and vanished on us."

After a ten-minute interrogation by Susan, Penny escaped to her room with the phone. She'd told Susan the truth, she'd seen no one but Zoe after the show, and had gone nowhere but home after their chat in the shop.

She dialed Zoe's number, fully expecting to reach her friend's grumpy grandmother, but Zoe answered after the first ring.

"Did the sheriff visit you yet?" Penny asked.

"Yeah," Zoe said. "It was weird. Grandma followed him outside when he tried to leave and wouldn't let him go for five minutes."

Zoe laughed, but it sounded uneasy.

"Did she get anything out of him?"

"Yeah," Zoe said. "I hid behind the door and listened. He thinks she ran away. Her parents just got divorced and her dad moved, so they think she ran off to live with him."

"Then why are they questioning people?"

"Because she's not the first to disappear," Zoe said.

"What?" This was the first Penny had heard of any disappearances, and she thought vanishing kids would probably count as big news in a small town like Dogwood.

"Not from here," Zoe continued. "A couple of girls from Kent, a boy from Yelm, and another girl from Lacy. They took someone in for questioning, but they let him go."

"Who?"

"Guess," Zoe said.

At first, Penny didn't have a clue, and then the answer hit her like a revelation.

"Tovar The Red," she said with certainty.

"Grandma threw a fit when the sheriff said they let him go, but they had to. He went straight to his room at the inn after the show, the desk clerk saw him come in, and he was there all night. They would have seen him leave."

"So maybe she did run away," Penny said.

"Yeah, probably," Zoe said.

"I'll call you back in a bit," Penny said. "Stay by the phone if you can so your grandma won't hang up on me."

"She's not here now," Zoe said. "She's at the diner gossiping to anyone who'll listen to her."

Penny said goodbye, hung up, and started downstairs—relieved, a little, by the information Zoe's grandma had coaxed out of Sheriff Price.

Now to convince Susan there was no reason to worry. Otherwise, Penny was apt to be spending quite a few boring hours pent-up in the house.

Only a few months ago that wouldn't have bothered her, but now she had a friend, and they had Aurora Hollow.

Chapter 13

The Face in the Mirror

The next few weeks dragged by in a haze of boredom.

Far from being relieved at the news that Jodi Lewis was a suspected runaway, and probably not a kidnapping, Susan abolished the newfound freedom Penny had enjoyed since leaving the city. Her bike leaned unused against the front porch, and Penny rode to school in the Falcon every morning.

Susan forbade her to leave the school grounds at lunchtime. And she spent the few hours after school let out and before the shop closed stuck inside with nothing more exciting than homework to occupy her. Zoe was with her for those few hours most days, but it was still idle time.

By the end of the second week, when Tovar The Red had not shown his face in town again and no more kids vanished, Susan began to relax and let Penny out after school, extracting a promise that she would not leave their property.

"I know you and Zoe have your own place back there somewhere," she said, nodding in the general direction of the high, wild field. "When I was your age there was a grove out there I used to play in. I went looking for it again but couldn't find it. I suppose it's overgrown now."

Penny suppressed a smile at this.

"We've gone down to the creek, but mostly we just hang out in the field."

No sooner than Susan allowed Penny to leave the house again, Zoe's curmudgeonly grandmother surprised them with an unexpected request. It came in the form of a letter, delivered by a thoroughly excited Zoe.

Penny and Zoe waited anxiously while Susan read the note, looking increasingly incredulous. After refolding and replacing it back in the envelope Zoe had handed her, she looked at the pair of them, her mildly chagrined expression fading into an indulgent smile.

"Tell her I said that would be just fine. We have enough room for one more."

Penny at least knew what the chagrined look was about—Zoe's grandma was part of a clique of grim-faced town ladies who remembered Penny's mom and Susan from when they were teenagers. She had branded them, and Penny by association, unrepentant troublemakers.

This still puzzled Penny, who had never seen that side of her mom or Susan. The woman she'd grown up with had been predictably boring, reliable to a fault.

One of these days, she'd work up the guts to ask Susan what kind of mischief they'd gotten up to as teenagers.

Zoe's grandma and a handful of her fellow curmudgeons were taking a two-week trip to Vegas; Zoe's mother, who was supposed to have come back to town for that short time, had canceled her trip back.

This put Susan in the unique position to be able to deny one of the women she referred to as 'The Town Elders.' However, she'd squashed the impulse for Penny's sake—and because she liked Zoe, if not her grandmother.

Penny refrained, barely, from running to Susan and

bowling her over in a tackle-hug. She could not stop a pleased squeal, which Zoe mimicked.

"Thanks, Susan!" Penny and Zoe shrieked in unison.

Susan only laughed and waved them off.

"I'll drive you home so you can tell her I said yes and pack some clothes. I just don't feel right letting you ride back to town alone. Especially in the dark."

Penny rolled her eyes behind Susan's back, making Zoe break into fresh laughter.

Susan spun around, as if she'd grown eyes in the back of her head and seen Penny's mockery.

"You," she said, pointing a finger at Penny and startling her into jumping back a step, "do your chores while we're gone."

Five minutes later Penny was alone, wiping down the kitchen counters before sweeping. Never in her life had Penny been so enthusiastic during her house chores.

It was Friday evening, Susan's overprotective grasp had loosened for the first time since Jodi Lewis's disappearance, the weekend stretched free and clear before her, full of freedom and possibilities, and now her best friend would be staying with her for the next two weeks.

For the first time since attending Tovar The Red's show at the park, life was good.

In less than thirty minutes, Penny finished her chores and Zoe came back with a huge duffel bag filled to seam-stretching capacity.

Susan offered Zoe a guest room on the second floor, one of the unused rooms haphazardly furnished with decades-old furniture not yet rickety enough to throw out.

"Most of the stuff in there was mine when I was your age. The bed, the dresser, the curtains." She pointed to a vanity on the opposite wall, and a large wooden chest on the floor beside it. "You can sleep here if you want. I thought you'd probably want to stay in Penny's room, but this one is open if you get tired of her."

They carried Zoe's stuff up to the attic room and Zoe unpacked, stowing her clothes, books, and her favorite rocks—the ones she simply couldn't be parted with—in the spare dresser.

Dinner was tacos. Susan cooked and seasoned the meat while Penny and Zoe grated cheese, shredded lettuce, and diced tomatoes.

After dinner, they sat quietly for a while watching Susan's pick for movie night, a regular Friday evening event, passing a bowl of popcorn between the three of them. The movie was a little too sappy for Penny's tastes, and so her attention kept drifting.

When it drifted to Zoe, her heart did a little flip-flop behind her ribs.

Zoe ignored the movie too. Her attention was focused on a shining oval object lying in her cupped hands.

Her souvenir mirror from Tovar's show—The Conjuring Glass.

Penny waited a few moments for her heart rate to return to something approaching normal, then forced a little cough to draw Zoe's attention. When that didn't work, she sidled over closer to Zoe and gave her ankle a jab with the toe of her shoe.

Zoe looked up, startled and blinking like someone caught napping.

Penny jerked her head in the direction of the hallway and rose. "Think I'm going to get ready for bed, Susan."

"Yeah," Zoe said, and yawned. "Me too. Goodnight."

"Goodnight girls," Susan said, her eyes never leaving the screen. This Friday night's hunk of a leading man was currently gazing deeply into the eyes of a breathless, young leading lady, and Susan, it seemed, didn't want to miss the juicy part of the scene.

Penny waited at the top of the stairs for Zoe to catch up.

"Don't let Susan see that," she pointed at the mirror in Zoe's hand. "She's freaked out about Tovar already. If she sees that and figures out where you got it...Zoe, what's wrong?"

Zoe looked frightened for a moment, on the cusp of panic. She cringed at the mirror, as if a large spider had just crawled onto her hand.

Then she shoved the mirror in her pants pocket, rubbing the palm of her hand against her jeans afterward, as if scrubbing off some unseen filth. Afterward, Zoe fixed a tired, resigned gaze on Penny.

"I need to talk to you, Penny. Something is going on. Something scary. I don't know what exactly, but it has something to do with this," she pointed a finger at the bulge the mirror made in her pocket. "It has something to do with *him*."

There was no need to ask who Zoe meant by *him*.

Penny sat on the edge of her bed, and Zoe sat on the edge of hers, shifting as she pulled the mirror from her pocket and set it next to Penny. After a slight hesitation, she flipped it upside down, as if afraid to look into the reflective surface.

"That night after the magic show I took the mirror out and stared into it. I thought maybe if you were looking into yours, we'd see each other in them again. I thought maybe we could even use them to talk to each other."

Penny's first thought was: *yes, I bet we could if we knew how*. Her second thought was: *but I didn't see her. I saw him*.

Had Penny told Zoe about that? She supposed not.

Penny hadn't looked into the mirror that night. She had shoved it into the bottom of her nightstand drawer, and had not moved it since.

"What did you see?"

"A bird." Zoe shivered, then continued. "A giant bird's head. When I saw it, it turned and stared back at me. Its eyes were red, like they were on fire."

"A bird?"

Zoe nodded.

"It looked at me, then it turned and walked away. It was huge…it walked like a person…it had arms and legs and wings. Then it vanished…and…"

The look Zoe shot at Penny was terrified, but not just terrified. She thought there was real shame in it too.

Embarrassment?

"What?"

For a moment, Zoe seemed unable to finish. She opened her mouth, her deeply tanned cheeks flushing a deeper red. There was some residual fear there, Penny thought, but the greater part of her discomfort was pure shame.

"Come on, Zoe. I won't laugh."

Zoe closed her eyes, leaned in close to Penny, and whispered.

At first, Penny thought Zoe was pulling her leg. Then Zoe moved away, opening her eyes again, and Penny knew she was not.

"What did you do?"

"I ran," Zoe said. "Out the back door, got on my bike, and just rode. I was almost out of town before I realized where I was going. I rode around town until it was too cold to stay out, then I snuck back in and slept in the living room."

"Did you tell your grandma?"

"Are you kidding?" Zoe actually laughed at the idea, though Penny didn't hear much honest humor in the laugh.

"She'd either call me a liar and ground me, or think I'd gone crazy and ship me to the closest lunatic asylum."

"Oh," Penny managed, feebly.

"I don't know if you've noticed, but she doesn't like having me around that much. You should hear her talk sometimes." Zoe scrunched up her face in a gargoyle-like caricature of wizened crotchetiness. "It's all that Indian's fault. I knew when your momma married him there would be nothing good from it. And now she's gone off to drive a truck with him and I have another kid to raise." She never says his name, he's just *that Indian*."

Penny felt a rush of anger for Zoe's grandmother, but held her tongue.

"Grandma never did like Dad, and she's given up trying to like me, I think. She's just counting the days until they come back for me."

A long silence unwound itself following that pronouncement. Penny just couldn't find the right words to break it. Finally, Zoe did.

"You're the only one I told," she said, her voice dropping to a near whisper again. "Who else would believe me?"

"Why do you keep looking at it then?"

Zoe shrugged, reached over, and picked the mirror up again, glanced into the reflective glass quickly, then turned it upside down on the palm of her hand. "I don't know. I just keep looking. I can't help it."

"Jodi Lewis had one," Penny said. "Just like ours, remember? She was one of the first onstage that night."

Zoe nodded. "I know."

Penny thought about the face she'd seen staring back at her through her own mirror and shuddered.

Zoe looked into hers again, longer and deeper this time, her gaze seeming to almost fall into it.

"It doesn't mean *he* took her though," Penny said.

Zoe looked up from the reflective glass again, catching Penny's eyes with her own. She did not reply or dispute Penny's words though. She didn't need to.

Zoe climbed into her bed, lying on her side to face Penny, and Penny did the same, pulling the sheets up underneath her chin and scooting to the edge closest to Zoe so they could resume their conversation.

Her words to Zoe, *It doesn't mean he took her*, played back in her mind; chased around and around in a circle by the words she'd spoken—shouted really—at Susan a few weeks before.

What did he do that was so bad?

Susan's reply came back to her, making her stomach tighten, making her feel sick.

"Penny?"

"What?"

"How did your mom die?"

The question jolted Penny, but after a few seconds consideration she realized that every time their conversations turned toward Penny's past or Penny's mother, she had quickly deflected. She didn't like talking or thinking about it. It was still painful. But Zoe was her friend. She knew almost everything about Zoe, and Zoe knew very little about her.

It's mine, Penny thought with uncharacteristic avarice. *My past … my pain, and I don't want to share it*!

Penny understood better than ever before why her mom had been so reluctant to share her past, her pain—and she understood why it was wrong to not share.

"If you don't want to talk about it you don't have to," Zoe said, sounding shamed.

"No, it's okay." Another long moment passed before Penny continued. "She worked for a talent agency and she had to travel a lot between San Francisco and L.A. The agency used a private jet. She was over the ocean when the engine failed."

Zoe said nothing for a while, waiting to see if Penny had finished.

"I'm sorry," Zoe said at last.

There was no more conversation that night. Within a few minutes, Zoe's light snores filled the room.

Strangely enough, Penny felt better after the telling. As if by sharing the story she was also sharing her pain. It was a feeling she wished her mom could have experienced with her.

It felt good to share.

Penny moved to the other side of her bed, reaching for the lamp, then moving to the top drawer of her nightstand. She slid it open slowly, not wanting the scrape and squeak of the warped wood to wake her friend.

She searched blindly until she found her mirror, then steeled herself, and brought it up before her face.

Her own reflection stared back at her.

Penny let out a long breath, closed the drawer, turned off the lamp on the nightstand, and then lay down to sleep.

She drifted off minutes later with the mirror clutched in her hand, and Zoe's whispered words echoing in her sleeping mind. The words she'd been too afraid to say aloud.

My closet door opened and something huge came out of it.

Penny awoke once to the bump and scratch of something against wood. A mouse in the wall maybe, but it sounded too big to be a mouse. It came again once, then no more, and she slept again.

Sometime during the night a teenage girl, who still had the wilted bouquet of flowers a handsome magician had given her a few weeks earlier, vanished. There at bedtime, gone the next morning.

Neither Penny nor Zoe found out until much later the next day, but they both awoke with a feeling that something bad had happened.

Chapter 14

The Door

They left for the hollow early the next morning, after a hastily eaten breakfast of eggs and toast. Susan was still asleep when they left, so Penny left her a note.

Susan,

Zoe and I are going out. We promise not to leave the property. Maybe we'll look for that old grove you told me about.

We'll check in around noon.

Love ya,

Penny

The sun was barely up when they'd finished breakfast, and had only just crested the eastern horizon when they walked into the lower field. They were used to sleeping in on weekends, so they felt strange being up and out with the rising sun. Sleeping in would have been impossible that morning after the nightmares that had plagued them that night.

They had awakened at the same time, both bolting upright. Before the feeble glow of dawn's approaching light could burn the full horror of their dreams away, they faced each other, and Penny spoke a single word.

Birdman.

The dream itself faded quickly, until all she could remember of it was feathery darkness and the slamming of a door.

When asked, Zoe said she couldn't remember anything from hers.

They walked quietly for a while, wallowing in the shared gloom of the morning, but as they climbed the rise to the higher, wilder field above, their spirits lifted.

The top of the hollow was in sight, and knowing they would shortly be back at their place after a forced absence of two weeks cheered them.

Penny had decided to keep the wand with her from now on, at least until the shadow that had fallen over Dogwood lifted. She didn't like leaving it behind. It made her feel vulnerable.

"Have you seen Ronan around at all?"

Zoe's question broke the crisp, autumn morning silence, startling Penny.

"No, I'm kind of hoping he'll be around. Maybe he knows what's going on," and since conversation had finally started again, Penny decided to tell Zoe something she should have already told her. She'd held her tongue for personal reasons.

Despite what Susan had said, Penny couldn't get the idea that Tovar The Red might be her father out of her head. Even if he wasn't her father, she was sure there was a connection between them. Penny was determined to uncover it, whatever it was. She would not allow herself to think that Tovar might have had anything to do with Jodi Lewis's disappearance.

He couldn't have, an inner voice argued. *He never left his room that night. He had an alibi, that's why they had to let him go.*

A second voice, not hers, but one that sounded like Ronan, replied with cynical humor.

Convenient, aye, Little Red? Very convenient.

What is that supposed to mean?

He's a magician, Ronan's voice spoke in her head, then retreated.

"Zoe?"

"Yeah?"

"During the show, when we looked in the mirrors ..."

Zoe stopped walking, regarded her curiously.

"You saw me in the mirror, right?" Penny asked.

"Yes," Zoe said, her curiosity becoming bewilderment.

"I didn't see you."

Penny told her what, who, she had seen staring back at her in the mirror.

After a moment Zoe asked, "What do you think it means?"

"I don't know," Penny said. "Maybe it was because I wanted to see him."

They started walking again, and when Zoe's silence held, Penny asked, "What do you think it means?"

"You're not going to like it," she said with a sad certainty.

"Tell me anyway."

"I think Tovar and The Birdman are working together."

There was another silence—that morning seemed to be full of uncomfortable silences, Penny reflected—and Zoe broke it.

"You mad at me now?"

"No," Penny said. She was a little mad though. She couldn't help it.

"Do you still want to find out? Do you still want to talk to him?"

"Yes."

Zoe offered no reply to this, and it was just as well. Nothing she could have said would have changed Penny's mind.

They both felt the magic of the place as they descended into Aurora Hollow—a tingling in their fingertips, a high buzz of energy that seemed to saturate them, and their excitement grew, pushing the nagging question of Tovar The Red and The Birdman out of their heads. A little, anyway.

They had never felt it this strongly before.

They hoped to see Ronan, either lounging in the mouth of his little cave or on one of the high boughs of the big tree at the water's edge.

Ronan was not there, but something else was. Something new.

"Look!" Penny pointed to the new thing, standing between two trees beyond the fire pit.

A door, old and weathered, standing there for no reason either girl could fathom.

Zoe strode to the door without hesitation or fear, inspecting the front, then walking around it. When she was standing before it again, she grasped the knob and turned it. The doorknob gave a faint rusty, dusty sigh when she turned it, then she pulled the door open.

Trees stood behind the opening. Trees and nothing else. She walked through it, then around to the front again, faced Penny, and raised her hands palms up, as if to say *I don't get it*.

"How did it get there?" Penny wondered aloud.

"You've got me," Zoe responded. She seemed torn between amusement and concern. "Ronan, maybe?"

"Maybe," Penny said. But there was no way to know for

sure until they saw him again, so Penny decided to try not to think about it too much. They had come here to practice.

"Come on, Zoe. Let's practice."

The next hour of ineffectual bangs and other accidental magic proved how out of practice they were. They improved during their second hour, and by the time they were ready to leave, Penny felt as if they were not just back on track, but gaining.

Penny, pointing the wand at her shoes, had levitated

herself a full ten feet off the ground before nerves had forced her back to the earth. Zoe, who had practiced the irritatingly slow growth spell on the overhead willow boughs almost every time they had visited the hollow before their forced hiatus, finally saw the results of her work. They were thicker and greener than ever, almost completely blocking out the sky overhead.

Zoe was also getting better at casting fire, and if she was quick enough, could catch the little red sliver she'd cast in midair and hold it until it had bloomed into a full-fledged fireball. Penny tried duplicating that trick and succeeded only in setting half a dozen small fires in the underbrush.

As always, they consulted the book again before they left, and as always found nothing new.

Zoe shouted in exasperation. "Ah! This is getting old!"

Penny commiserated. "How do we tell if someone else can even join?"

Zoe considered this for a moment, then grinned, her anger departed. "If they can see Ronan, they can join."

An idea so simple and so obvious, there was no use trying to reason it out or pick it apart. All Penny could do was return Zoe's smile and agree.

"Where is he?"

"Beat's me," Zoe said.

They stored the chest inside the hollowed out portion of the big tree, but packed the wand and the book in Zoe's empty bag.

They were up the slope and halfway across the high field before they heard the voices shouting their names from down below.

"*Penny*! *Zoe*!" Susan and someone else.

Exchanging startled looks, they jogged the rest of the way across the field of high, wild grass. Before they reached the decline to the lower field, the top of a brown-haired head appeared, and Susan's employee Jenny topped the slope, looking frantic.

She saw them, and her face relaxed. "Up here! I found them!"

Susan appeared only seconds later, puffing as she raced up the steep incline, then dropped to her knees before Penny and Zoe.

Penny braced herself for some serious shouting. What she was not prepared for was for Susan to drop to her knees and seize both her and Zoe in long and crushing hugs.

"What?"

Susan, tears streaming from red and puffy eyes, did not answer.

Jenny did.

"There was another disappearance last night," she said. "We found out a little while ago, and when we couldn't find you …"

She didn't need to finish. Penny understood. She also understood that her restored freedom was at an end—and was doubly thankful that Zoe was staying with her, at least for the next few weeks, and that they had decided to bring their wand and the book back this time.

Part of her wanted Zoe to go home though. Her friend's unwelcome suspicion about Tovar The Red, the man Penny was convinced was her long lost father, festered, growing into resentment.

Lying in their beds that night, Penny drifting on the edge of sleep, Zoe spoke.

"They'll never find him," she said.

"Yeah they will." Penny injected all the confidence she could into her reply. "They have to."

"They won't. They don't know where to look," Zoe said.

"For all we know he's five hundred miles away."

Penny considered this, decided it could be true, and wondered how many other kids from other towns The Birdman had taken.

"I'll talk to Tovar when he comes back. It can't be a coincidence, him coming at the same time as The Birdman."

Zoe said nothing.

"He might know something about it. He might be able to help."

"What if he doesn't come back? They did try to arrest him."

Penny sat up until she could see Zoe leaning against her stack of pillows. "He'll come back. Susan said they used to come here for Harvest Days all the time. He'll come back."

To see me, if nothing else, Penny dared to hope.

For several seconds they were silent, then Penny said, "We're going to have to tell someone what you saw."

"No one would believe us, and even if they did, no one could catch him," Zoe said. "For all we know he flies away."

For that, Penny had no rebuttal.

The next lag in conversation stretched, and Penny was about to ask Zoe what she thought they should do, when her friend's soft snores sounded.

Penny closed her eyes and let exhaustion take her.

In her dream, Penny stood in Aurora Hollow watching the door, colored blood red by a low-burning fire. A flash of bright, white light shone through the creases where the door wasn't perfectly flush inside its frame. Then the door flew open, and a dark shape, half-bird and half-man, blocked out the perfect rectangle of bright white light.

Penny bolted upright on her bed, the light of a new sunrise throwing dusty motes over her, half blinding her. And when a new shape rose to block it from her eyes, she was half-convinced The Birdman had followed her from her dream.

"*What*?" It was Zoe, sitting up in her bed, startled and wide-eyed. "*What's wrong*?"

Penny felt the sweat of fear, tacky and cool on her forehead, begin to dry.

"Nothing," she said. "Sorry."

Zoe slid back onto the bed and appeared to go back to sleep, and Penny imitated her. She did not sleep again that morning though. She only lay there, her eyes closed, wishing the dream's afterimages would fade from her mind's eye.

Later that day, Penny heard rumors at school that another girl from another nearby town had vanished in the night.

The town held its breath for the next few days. There was school, where Penny's fellow students wandered the halls between classes in subdued groups and pairs. Parents volunteered as hall and playground monitors and herded the children like sheep every moment of the day. No one else from Dogwood disappeared in that time, but two kids, a twin brother and sister, did vanish from their home in Auburn the night before.

"I don't know why they're bothering," Penny heard Katie West say to her small group of friends once, while they all waited for their parents to pick them up and take them home. "Nothing's going to happen during the day. It doesn't matter what they do. It's the dark they should worry about."

Then she noticed Penny and Zoe standing close enough to hear her conversation, and led her friends away, throwing a scowl over her shoulder. The scowl seemed halfhearted though, more habit than hate.

"What does she have against us anyway?" Penny asked Zoe, not really expecting an answer.

She got one anyway.

Katie turned and stalked toward them, an expression of

lazy contempt on her face. For a moment, Penny thought Katie was going to hit her, and she had a crazy impulse to pull her wand, but Katie stopped a few feet short and faced Penny, hands on her hips.

"Your whole family is trouble, Little Red. Every single one of them, and you're just as bad."

Penny had no response. She simply stood agape.

"Yeah, I know all about you guys. Your mom and your aunt." Penny's shocked silence seemed to enrage Katie further, and her voice rose to a shout. "My dad told me all about them when he found out you came back. He told me what happens to people who get mixed up with your family."

Penny's shocked silence broke. "What are you talking about? What did my mom ever do to ..."

Katie didn't wait for her to finish.

"Ask Susan about Tracy West sometime. Ask her why Tracy had to leave town. Then you'll know what I have against you!" That said, Katie turned, joining her friends, leaving Penny standing in a sea of curious rubberneckers.

"She's crazy," Zoe marveled. "Absolutely bug-eyed."

Penny said nothing, but thought she understood. Her mom's friend Tracy, who had left town never to return after the accident, was Katie's aunt. It was a revelation she wasn't ready to share with Zoe yet, because sharing that would mean having to share a whole lot more.

The next morning, after getting ready for school, Penny found Susan on the phone looking shaken and tired. A third town girl had disappeared. It was Katie West.

Chapter 15

The Wrong Boogeyman

The day Katie disappeared, Penny and Zoe heard gossip at school that the sheriff was going to cancel Harvest Days. Penny wasn't surprised, but she was disappointed. She'd been looking forward to the fair week.

That night at home she overheard Susan on the phone with Jenny, saying Penny might be safer back in San Francisco at the group home until they caught the kidnapper.

A few months earlier this would have been welcome, but now it made her feel like shouting and crying simultaneously.

That night another kid went missing; a boy Penny remembered very vaguely from the magic show in the park. This time there was a bit of good news to balance out the bad.

Sheriff Price had a suspect in custody, and expected to find the missing kids soon.

The gossip was unspecific, and Penny went through the day in a daze of confused anticipation, wanting to believe they had managed to catch The Birdman, but not quite able to. She just could not imagine some small-town sheriff, elected more because of family influence than any flair for crime fighting according to Susan, stopping such an exotic and frightening foe.

That evening they watched the television, channel surfing from one news program to the next, hoping for some scrap of information. There was nothing beyond vague references at first, short teasers that sent Susan into uncharacteristic cursing tirades.

At last, the local station rewarded them with a full story.

They watched live, as the sheriff stood on the steps of the town's courthouse, armed guards flanking the door. They could hear the angry shouts of off camera parents and townspeople, and Penny thought the guards were there more to keep the citizens from lynching the imprisoned man than to keep him from escaping.

"I wonder who they got," Penny said, exchanging a meaningful glance with Zoe.

"Hush," Susan barked, and Penny hushed at once.

Sheriff Price spoke.

"Early this morning, following the reported abduction of a fourth child from Dogwood, we received an anonymous tip naming Gregory Hicks, formerly of Puyallup. Mr. Hicks has moved from city to city, staying at campgrounds since retiring from his job at a Puyallup mill last spring. We arrived later in the morning with a warrant, and found personal items belonging to some of the missing children in Mr. Hicks's camper."

A volley of questions followed, during which Sheriff Price merely stood closed-mouthed and still as a statue, arms crossed over his chest.

Penny took advantage of the moment to venture a question. "Where is Puyallup?"

"Shhh," Susan said, pressing a finger to her lips.

After a few moments, the reporters decided there would be no answers to their questions, and settled for Sheriff Price to continue his statement.

"While we haven't yet located the missing children, we believe it's only a matter of time."

Angry babble from the crowd rose again, but Sheriff Price pressed on, raising his voice to be heard.

"In the meantime, I'd like to squelch rumors that our city council has decided to cancel Harvest Days. Nothing—" he had to shout to make his voice heard, "We will find our missing children, and *nothing* would please me more than to welcome them back in celebration."

With that, the sheriff stepped back from the microphone, raised his hands, palm out to forestall any further questions—not that it did any good, the questions rained at him fast and furious—and retreated past the armed deputies guarding the door. A few of the bolder reporters tried to follow him, still firing questions, but the deputies blocked them.

The scene in front of the town courthouse vanished, replaced by the ever-grinning face of the anchor, saying Hicks had no family, no job, and that he was a wanderer, moving from town to town and living out of his camper. Running in a column to her left, top to bottom, were photos of the missing kids, and to her right, a photo of Gregory Hicks.

Hicks was an old man with flyaway white hair, dark sunken eyes, and a narrow, scarecrow face.

Penny thought if you looked up the word *boogeyman* in the dictionary, you'd find his picture next to the definition. He certainly looked the part of the kidnapping boogeyman.

He was innocent, and Penny knew it.

Susan turned the television off, and blew out a gusty sigh of relief. For several moments there was utter silence in the living room.

"Do you think they'll find them?" Zoe asked.

Susan looked at her, distracted, and Penny thought her relieved expression tensed just a bit.

"I hope so," she said. Then, with a little more conviction, "I'm sure they will. I'm just glad I don't have to worry about you two now."

Penny forced a smile of her own. "Yeah, me too."

Penny herself was very worried. She was worried enough for the both of them.

"We have to do something," Zoe said as Penny tried, but failed to go to sleep.

"I know," Penny said. "Not yet though."

"What?" Zoe's disbelief was clear in her voice. "Are you kidding me? After tonight, you know they won't catch … *him*."

"Yes, you're right. But right now we don't need to worry about him kidnapping anyone else. At least not for a while," she hastened to add before Zoe could argue again. "Who do you think tipped the sheriff off? Who do you think planted that stuff in his camper?"

"You think it was Tovar?"

"No," Penny said. She knew her certainty was irrational, but she knew, just knew, that if Tovar was involved, he would be on her side.

Maybe that was why he had come, to catch The Birdman.

"I think it was The Birdman, and I think he's coming here for us. But not yet."

"What about Tovar?"

Penny grimaced.

"He'll be back for Harvest Days. We'll talk to him then. This time," she said grimly, "we won't let him get away."

"And what do we do about The Birdman?"

"We wait until the fair starts," Penny said. "Then we'll

call him out."

"Oh, good," Zoe said without enthusiasm. "Sounds like a great plan to me."

Though she didn't say so aloud, Penny couldn't help but agree. She wasn't thrilled with the idea either, yet what other choice did they have? They could wait for The Birdman to come for them, or they could go after him.

There were only three days left of the school week, then the weekend and the week-long fair. Only three days, but those three days seemed to drag.

The town seemed wrapped in a bubble of nervousness. The relief at having a suspect locked safely away, a suspect that appeared doubly guilty when the disappearances stopped, was a short-lived relief. The children were still missing, and the silence from the Sheriff's Office suggested that there was no progress in finding them.

Parents of the missing kids appeared on local television on Wednesday, giving separate interviews; on Thursday night they were together, speaking out on a national show that promised to bring their cases all the attention they could stand.

On Friday, Main Street became a parade of news vans and strangers behind microphones and cameras, which, Penny supposed, is what the parents of the missing children wanted. They tacked and taped posters to every available surface in town, each with a different and hauntingly familiar face. There was Katie; the boy, Joseph; Amber, the teenage girl who kept breaking out in flowers during the magic show; and Jodi, the first to vanish.

The reporters broadcast their faces all over the country, and everyone would watch for them, hoping for the ten seconds of fame any rescuer would receive.

Not a bad plan, Penny thought—but in this case, she knew it wouldn't work.

The night of Friday, September 29th came, and with nine school-free days stretching out before them, Penny and Zoe snuck out of the house just before midnight.

More than anything else, they needed to practice their magic. The Birdman would come for them soon. They could only hope they would be ready when he did.

They felt none of the usual anticipation as they crested the slope to the wild stretch of land leading to Aurora Hollow, only a sense of hopelessness, almost a feeling of doom.

Zoe clutched the wand at her side, itching for the small comfort of firelight the old stone pit would at least offer, and dreading the first of a new series of practice sessions just as much. As much as they reviewed the spells they had learned, they could find nothing they considered a practical offensive spell in their current repertoire, only things that seemed moderately useful at best, and downright silly on the whole.

There was the modified fire spell Zoe had succeeded in casting on their last visit to the hollow, but it was too unsure. Zoe just didn't know if she could pull it off when the time came.

Zoe had a hunch, a hope she'd shared with Penny, that they might be able to create the right spell, the magical equivalent of throwing rocks at The Birdman, but only if it was a simple one.

Penny was hopeful too, but not at all convinced.

They'd just have to see.

"I hope Ronan is there tonight. I bet he could help," Zoe said.

"Yeah. Me too."

Ronan's frequent absences, days, sometimes as much as a

week at a time, were nothing new to them—but they hadn't seen him for almost a month. They thought he might come to visit them sometime to find out why they weren't coming around, but he did not.

Penny was worried for him. The last time she'd seen him was just before the first kidnapping. What if The Birdman had attacked him, hurt him, or carried him off to wherever he kept the missing children?

From that, her thoughts turned back to the mysterious door, a door that didn't belong there, but was there nonetheless. It had appeared about the same time Ronan had disappeared. There was a connection, she was sure, but didn't know what it was.

Which one had put it there, Tovar or The Birdman, and why?

The question that concerned them most however was how to keep from joining the ranks of the missing.

They arrived at the drop to the hollow and descended in silence, Penny leading, and Zoe following closely with the wand held in her fist.

Ronan did not emerge from the mouth of his cave, or leap down from the upper branches of his favorite tree to greet them.

Neither did The Birdman.

Zoe lit the fire and they stood over it for a few minutes, feeding it with dead limbs they had scavenged on previous visits.

"Might as well start," Penny said a few minutes later.

"Yeah," Zoe said glumly, and began searching for a suitable target while Penny stood back and considered the door. Zoe returned a few minutes later dragging a length of deadwood behind her, which she set up against the vertical part of the bank a few feet away from the steep path.

Penny considered and rejected a half-dozen booby trap

plans as too complicated or too chancy, and decided to shelve that idea. There was no way to tell which direction he would come from anyway, if he flew in.

She turned her attention back to Zoe, and found her friend red-faced with concentration, wand pointing at her target.

"Any luck?"

For a moment, Zoe continued to glare at the dead tree trunk she'd placed against the stone and dirt, the wand shaking in her hand, then she lowered it and shook her head.

"Nothing," she said sourly. "We might as well yell at it."

"We'll figure something out," Penny offered in what she hoped was a confident tone.

Penny took a turn with the wand, only having the vaguest idea of what she wanted to do. After a few hours of switching off, they decided to call it a night. Frustrated as they were, they were just too tired to continue.

They came back the next morning, Susan relenting only after they had promised to check in every few hours. They took turns again: Penny with the wand, practicing every spell she knew and hoping to find some practical way to use one of them against The Birdman, and Zoe pouring over every word the book had shown them up to that point.

They returned to the house before lunch, left for the hollow again that afternoon, and snuck out again late that night.

They followed the same schedule the next day, and ended the third late night with no more progress than they had the first.

Reluctantly, Zoe agreed that they should focus more on using what they did know in new ways.

The next day, the first school-free Monday since the end of summer, marked the start of Harvest Days, and the return of Tovar The Red.

Part 3

The Conjuring Glass

Chapter 16

The House of Mirrors

Penny and Zoe rode into town Monday morning with Susan to watch the carnies and a few hired locals set up the fair. It was like something out of a book or movie: the entire town transforming into a carnival. Local businesses put up colorful bunting and moved displays of their merchandise onto the sidewalks. The bakery just down the sidewalk from Sullivan's put a concession stand across the street in front of the park.

The park itself had already transformed. Usually sleepily empty, it bustled with a flurry of activity. Carnies setting up games, food stands, trinket stands, and rides.

The larger rides like the Ferris Wheel, the Octopus, the Zipper, and a single, short roller coaster sprawled over the park's border and into the school playground.

Large trucks occupied almost every inch of curb along the park side of Main Street, some relieved of their cargo, others still bearing the skeletal frames and gantries of rides yet to be set up.

There were even a half-dozen tents, mostly devoted to animals and performers.

One had a large poster board propped on an easel beside the closed front flap with a life-sized photo of Tovar The Red. If Susan saw that, she gave no sign. She advised them to stick to the games, stay clear of the rides under construction, and told them to check in every hour, on the hour.

"Have fun, girls," she said, and slipped them each a twenty. "If you have anything left, bring me some Elephant Ears from the concession stand."

"Elephant Ears," Penny repeated. Whatever they were, they sounded completely gross to Penny.

Susan patted her stomach. "Mmmm, good stuff, kiddo."

Zoe seemed surprised by Susan's casual display of generosity, and only stood there for a moment, staring at the money in her hand.

"C'mon." Penny grabbed her by the arm and dragged her across the street.

Their first stop was at the concession stand, where morbid curiosity alone compelled Penny to try what Susan called *Elephant Ears*.

"They're called scones," the girl at the stand said with obvious disapproval.

Penny found the scones, deep-fried batter with melted butter and powdered sugar, to be more than just *good stuff*. They were delicious. She shared them with Zoe as they wound in and out of completed stands and rides yet to be opened.

She kept her eyes open for Tovar's wild shock of flame red hair, but did not see it. Every few minutes she looked back over her shoulder to see if Susan was watching from the store's front window. Fortunately, with the influx of people visiting Dogwood for the fair, Susan was too busy monitoring customers.

Penny checked her watch—twenty minutes until it was time to check in.

"Wanna get tickets?"

They wound their way to the gazebo, now a ticket booth instead of a stage, and waited in line to spend the last of their cash. Zoe reminded Penny they needed to save enough to buy Susan's Elephant Ears. After getting their tickets, they stopped at the concession stand again, then dropped Susan's Elephant Ears at the shop.

The sheriff closed down Main Street; traffic detoured the three blocks from where the park began to where the school ended. Penny wondered briefly where the visitors were parking. The lane behind the Main Street shops had barely enough room for the people who worked along that stretch, let alone hundreds of visitors.

The growing flow of foot traffic seemed to be coming from the direction of the school, so she supposed they were using the school's parking lot.

Susan was busy with a steady stream of customers at the cash register, but she acknowledged Penny with a smile and thumbs up when they took her scones to the break room.

On their way back across the crowded street Penny said, "Let's check out his tent."

"What if he's in there?" Zoe asked, startled.

I hope he is, Penny almost said, but she bit the reply back. A flash of anger filled her at the realization that Zoe, despite all of her rationalizations and belief, still thought Tovar was working with The Birdman.

For a moment Penny questioned her belief. Not a

rational one, she knew, but purely emotional. She squashed the dissenting thoughts quickly.

Penny had kept her flier from the magic show hidden away in her dresser—not even Zoe knew she had it—and had compared it with the single photo of her father so many times there was now no doubt in her mind at all.

If Tovar was not her father, then maybe he was an uncle.

She refused to believe Tovar was the kidnapper.

"You have the wand, right?" Penny asked.

"Yeah," Zoe said, indicating the inside pocket of the light jacket she wore against the cool and overcast autumn day.

The sea of bodies thinned as they neared Tovar's tent, which stood at the very perimeter of the park, almost by itself. As Penny grasped the closed door flap meaning to have a peek inside, she tensed with the expectation of discovery by one of the carnival folk.

No one yelled at them to get away. No one tried to stop her as she lifted the flap and poked her head inside.

"What's in there?" Zoe whispered, pressing in close for a look of her own. "Is he there?"

Penny withdrew with a sigh of disappointment.

"No. No one is in there. It's empty."

There was nothing. No stage, no seats, no changing room cordoned off at the far end of the large tent. Just darkness and empty space.

"We can check later," Zoe offered, but Penny clearly heard the relief in her voice, and was suddenly angry with her friend.

Keeping her lips pressed tightly together, Penny marched away toward the other tents. Zoe had to hurry to keep up.

"What's wrong?"

"Nothing," Penny said, but did not attempt to keep the coolness out of her voice.

They skirted the other tents, giving them no more than a cursory look, and started for the growing aisle of carnival booths.

"Hey!" Zoe grabbed Penny's arm, trying to stop her, but Penny jerked free and moved a little faster.

"Penny!" Zoe almost shouted this, and a few heads turned to regard them.

Penny stopped and barked, "What?"

The expression on Zoe's too pale face cooled Penny's anger.

Penny followed Zoe's pointing finger with her eyes and found what had startled, no, frightened her.

The House of Mirrors, which Penny had just passed.

A rope blocked the stairs to the latched door of the house, and a *closed* sign hung from it.

The false front on the House of Mirrors, which Penny had missed on her angry march past it, depicted a dark figure, some twenty feet tall, its head towering over them and staring down with eyes like black pearls floating in pools of blood.

A giant effigy of The Birdman.

Penny lost her residual anger in a flash of shock and fear. For a moment she couldn't even move, half convinced the giant birdman would leap from the false front of the House of Mirrors and descend upon them.

Someone bumped Penny while passing by, and Zoe grabbed her arm to steady her.

They faced each other, Zoe very pale, Penny standing on legs that felt like rubber. What Penny said next shocked even her.

"Let's go inside."

There was really no way to sneak, so they walked around to the back of the double-wide trailer as inconspicuously as they could.

Behind that last row of games, rides, and booths everything was still, almost silent. The busy babble of the Chehalis River competed with the noise of the park, but couldn't overcome it. The short run of fence that surrounded the House of Mirrors had a single locked gate at the back. They climbed over it and up the steps to the back door with a sign that said Emergency Exit over it.

Penny thought it would have to be unlocked—fire codes or some other city code would necessitate it—and it was.

With a final quick look to either side, Penny opened the door and led Zoe inside.

The room they stepped into was not a part of the mirror maze, but a short and narrow hallway lined with doors. There were five doors set frame-to-frame lining each side, and one at the end. The doorknobs were old tarnished brass, each filigreed with designs and symbols neither of them could read. Looking at them for more than a few seconds made Penny's eyes water and her head hurt. Beneath each doorknob was a large brass key plate.

The symbols and shapes seemed to move in the unsteady light. A single light bulb flickered overhead, making the girls' shadows dance across the dark wood of the doors like hyperactive silhouettes.

"Should we try them?" Penny asked, her hand hovering nervously inches away from the first door on her right.

Zoe rolled her eyes and grasped the first doorknob on the left.

It would not budge.

Zoe bent down and peered through the large keyhole.

"What's in there?"

"I don't know."

Penny tried a door to the same effect, then checked the keyhole. At first, there was nothing but solid blackness, but as she gripped the doorknob to pull herself up, the darkness lightened into a gray fog, then resolved itself into clearer shapes. A room of some kind, and a large one, but it was too dark to be certain what kind of room it was.

"Look again," Penny said, and when Zoe put her eye back to the keyhole, Penny guided her hand to the doorknob.

Zoe gasped and pressed her face in closer to the keyhole.

"What is it?"

She drew back a few inches, then pressed her eye to the keyhole again. "I can see myself. It's a big mirror."

This didn't seem particularly odd to Penny, they were in a house of mirrors after all. That room was probably storage for extra mirrors. She moved to the next door without comment, tried the doorknob, found it locked, and peered in through the keyhole. This, too, looked in on a large, dark room—yet not the same room the last keyhole looked in on. The doors were only inches apart, but opened on different rooms.

No, she realized. Not a room at all, but a cave. Long tapestries that hung the entire length on both sides gave it the appearance of a room, but the ceiling and far wall were both made of rough stone.

There was a door at the far end. Like the doors lining

the hallway, the door at the other end of that room had a tarnished brass doorknob and key plate. Unlike the others, there was a large oval mirror in a silver frame hung high up on it.

Looking too long at that mirror was worse than trying to read the symbols on the doorknobs. Its reflection fluctuated, showing the room it stood in, then other rooms, and sometimes transparent, ghostly faces. These images only half formed, then retreated too quickly for Penny to study.

Zoe looked in another keyhole and said she saw trees, and the next one Penny peeked through showed her what looked like a library, or a study. Bookshelves stuffed with dusty old volumes covered every wall of this room, and in the center was a single desk and companion chair.

Stranger by the second.

She moved down the hallway, trying all the doors, and was not surprised to find them all locked, except for the door at the end of the hallway. That door was identical to the others, same size and design, same almost-black wood, except that instead of the doorknob there was a simple handle.

Penny pulled it open and saw the other side was one long mirror, top to bottom, side to side, and designed to blend in almost seamlessly with the mirrored corridor.

Beyond this door was the real house of mirrors, deserted because it was not yet open. If they continued inside, they would eventually find their way out through the front. That wouldn't be a good idea, even though Penny was eager to explore it. She didn't know what kind of trouble they might get in if they were caught snooping around, and she didn't want to find out.

Zoe seemed to be thinking along the same lines. "Come

on, let's get out."

After integrating themselves back into the carnival goers, Penny and Zoe walked toward Tovar's tent. A small crowd had gathered around the front, converging on the poster board sign. Penny and Zoe forced their way to the front, and saw there was now a time for the first show stenciled on it in bold black letters.

The tent's flap was open, but roped off just inside, and a circular, raised stage stood in the center, surrounded by a ring of bleachers five seats high. One gap in the bleachers facing the tent's entrance provided access for the audience. Another gap at the other end facilitated a catwalk, which led from the stage to an old, tall safe box, like something you'd see in a Wild West movie about bank robbers.

Zoe grabbed Penny's arm, checked her watch, and said, "Fifteen minutes."

Penny did not need her to elaborate; she knew exactly what her friend meant.

Only fifteen minutes ago, this tent had been empty.

Now it was ready for the audience that would fill it that very evening—and too late in the day for Penny to go. She'd be back at home or practicing in the hollow when Tovar performed that night, and she knew that no amount of pleading would persuade Susan to let her stay for it.

"Time to check in," she grumbled, and wound her way out of the crowd, back toward the bookstore.

They spent the remainder of the morning playing games and watching the House of Mirrors, waiting for it to open.

They resisted the temptation to use the wand while losing spectacularly at the Ring Toss, Dart Throw, Test Your Strength, and Target Shooting. However, when the huckstering carnie at the Strike Booth laughed at Penny's first attempt to knock over a pyramid of lead pins, Zoe gave in to temptation. Penny felt the heat of a blush spread across her cheeks as she lobbed her second softball at the stacked lead pins, then gaped in amazement as the pins scattered. They flew in all directions.

While Penny walked away with her prize, a stuffed bear almost as big as she was, she saw the carnie examining the pin her ball had hit, running a finger across a deep dent in the solid lead.

"What did you do?" Penny asked when the booth was well behind them.

"Don't worry," Zoe said, sounding not even slightly abashed. "No one saw me."

"No," Penny said. "How did you do it?"

"It was hidden up my sleeve. I just got mad and thought about knocking them down…" Zoe stopped and faced Penny, a smile lighting her face.

Susan ran them home during her lunch break, and they spent the rest of the afternoon in the hollow practicing Zoe's simple, but effective, new spell.

Chapter 17

Inside the House of Mirrors

Penny and Zoe snuck out again just before midnight and made their way through another chilly October night to the hollow. The evidence of Zoe's earlier practice lay scattered around them: shattered driftwood logs, splintered deadwood, and blasted pinecones.

After starting a fire, further warming the already unseasonably warm atmosphere of the hollow, they gathered the remains of the wood and stoked the flame with it.

Tonight it was Penny's turn to practice while Zoe kept a lookout, watching her mirror for The Birdman.

Rather than forage for targets in the dark, Penny brought the stuffed bear she'd won from the snickering carnie at the Strike Booth and set the makeshift target against the dirt wall that bore the scars of Zoe's earlier practice session.

As she squared up about ten feet away from the dummy, readying herself, she spotted Zoe peering intently into her mirror beside the fire.

"Do you see him yet?"

Zoe shook her head. "I see something, but not him."

Penny let the wand tip drop and turned to Zoe. "What?"

"I'm not sure. I think it's a…" She looked up at Penny, an expression that might have signaled recognition on her face. "I think it's a door."

Penny considered this and wasn't surprised.

She raised her wand again and thought, *knock him down*. She gave a little mental push, and saw something that might have been a heat shimmer leave the wand tip. There was some recoil, but weak, forcing her wand hand up a few inches, and her spell struck the stuffed bear, caving its chest in with a sound of a fist striking a pillow.

That would barely ruffle his feathers, Penny thought, a little disappointed. *I'll have to do better than that*.

An hour later the stuffed bear lay torn and tattered on the ground, both eyes and one ear missing, and leaking stuffing from several tears and holes. Penny gave up trying to set it back up after each hit, and simply pummeled it where it lay. There was a foot-deep dent in the bank behind it, where a few of her spells missed and blasted away dirt and stone.

Better, Penny thought, and smiled.

"Want to trade?" Penny asked, and Zoe was happy to oblige.

"That was getting really boring. I was about to fall asleep."

Penny regarded Zoe for a few minutes, watched the stuffed bear come further apart under her friend's assault, then pulled her own mirror out of her pocket and stared into it.

She saw nothing unusual, no Birdman, no door, only

her own reflected face.

Tentatively she whispered, "Father?"

For a moment her own tired, hopeful face stared back at her. Then a fog covered it, and a new face formed in the fog. A pale shape at first, topped by wild, flyaway hair so red it could have been reflected fire from the circle of stones. Then the features resolved themselves, and the shocked, wary face of Tovar The Red stared up at her.

Penny glanced quickly at Zoe, found her hard at work blasting away at the dirt bank, and turned back to her mirror.

Whispering again, "Dad?"

Tovar's watchful expression relaxed into a grin that made his sharp features a little friendlier, and gave a slight nod. Before she could speak further, Tovar pressed a finger to his lips, mouthed the word, *later*, and vanished.

Zoe practiced for a while longer, and Penny watched the mirror, once again showing only her own reflection, until she started to nod off.

"Come on," Zoe said, rousing Penny as her eyes slipped closed. "Let's get back. I'm pooped."

Penny nodded and grabbed her arm before she could turn away. "I think we're ready now."

"Yeah," Zoe agreed, though she sounded less than enthusiastic. "We're as ready as we'll ever be."

The next day, Tovar's tent was gone. The life-sized poster board was gone, and Penny felt the bright secret hope that she'd get to meet him, to finally meet her father, depart.

Had something happened to him?

She gave no sign of her disappointment, and after a short search of the park grounds affirmed he had not simply moved his tent, they went to the House of Mirrors, which was now open.

The line was longer than those for the other rides, and hearing the conversation between Rooster, who for a wonder had not noticed them standing only a few feet behind him, and one of his friends, they had a good idea why.

"I don't know how they do it. Probably lasers or something."

"That's not lasers," his friend said, his tone confident and knowing. "It's holograms."

"My brother screamed like a girl when he came out," Rooster said, and laughed.

Behind them, a group of Katie West's friends laughed and flirted with a trio of boys passing by, looking like kings of the fair with their football letterman jackets. The tallest of the girls, her short brown hair streaked with blonde highlights, seemed to have stepped into the role as queen bee in Katie's absence. She continued the conversation they had been having before getting in line.

"Yeah, I hope they find her. I'm just sayin'…you know …I was kind of getting sick of her anyway."

"You gonna ditch her when she comes back?" one of her friends asked.

"*If* she comes back," the new queen bee said, and to Penny she sounded remarkably unconcerned.

Zoe tugged on Penny's arm, and she saw the line moving up. They moved with it, and she tried her hardest to ignore the rest of the conversation behind them. She didn't like Katie, but suddenly found herself feeling bad for the girl.

Other bits of conversation floated back to them.

"…My third time through. Scariest damn thing I've ever…"

"…It's like he could almost reach out and grab you!"

"I'm taking Ellen's phone in. I gotta' record this."

After a few minutes, they found themselves at the front of the line, and as the carnie ushered them through the rope gate and up the steps to the entrance, Penny had her first real moment of doubt. She froze inside the doorway, somebody behind them laughed, and Zoe shoved her in with a growl.

There was a moment of pure darkness after the batwing door swung closed behind them, and then the place filled with a strange, ambient light. There were no overhead lights. The only light was a soft glow that seemed to come from the mirrors themselves.

When Penny finally registered the image in the mirror directly before her, she gasped and spun around, searching for what she knew would not be there.

Zoe, who had been behind her only a few seconds before, was gone.

"Zoe?"

She waited for a reply, but heard nothing.

She spun in a circle, looking for a way out, but found her own reflection facing her from four directions. Reaching out slowly, her fingers brushed the cool surface of the mirrors to her right and to her left.

Something that was not a reflection of her moved quickly through the mirror in front of her, and she turned quickly to see it. There was nothing behind her except smooth, cold glass.

Taking a deep breath to control the panic that tried to bloom in her head, she turned again, reached out for what appeared to be her own reflection—and watched her hand reaching for her reflection's hand, but not stopping at the point where the mirror appeared to be. A trick of light and reflection? She didn't know, but she did breathe easier when she stepped forward and found a narrow, mirrored hallway on her right.

Penny knew this hallway was a trick of light, it seemed to go on forever, its end lost in darkness long after the double-wide trailer that contained the House of Mirrors would have ended. So she tried to ignore the unease that wanted to freeze her in place, and stepped forward.

"Zoe?"

Nothing.

"Anyone?"

No one.

Penny took another step forward and flinched to her left as something large and dark flashed by on her right.

There could be nothing else in the corridor with her and she knew it. The hall was far too narrow, but she had seen something reflected in the mirror for just a moment.

Maybe something *in* the mirror.

That was an idea she would have normally dismissed at once as stupid. However, in The Birdman's House of Mirrors, she could not push the idea away. There was magic here.

She took another step, looking right, looking left, and she stopped abruptly as her wide-eyed reflection stretched, changed, and became the image of her taller friend.

Zoe appeared to be looking back at her from inside the mirror—it was not just a separating pane of glass between them. There was no depth behind it, only Zoe's reflection—and there was no recognition in her dark, frightened eyes.

"Zoe!" She pounded a fist against the spotless surface, not caring if it shattered, not caring if she cut or embarrassed herself.

Zoe did not hear her, seemed completely oblivious to her presence. She looked forward again and took another step, and Penny saw that dark shape that had teased its way across her own peripheral vision maneuvered in behind her friend.

"Zoe, behind you!"

Penny rushed forward to keep up with Zoe, and as she passed a seam between one mirror and the next, The Birdman vanished. Zoe stopped, looked to her right, staring unknowingly at Penny again, then to her left. A second later, she turned and vanished.

A sound from behind caught Penny's attention, and she turned slowly, dreading what she might see, illusion or not.

The Birdman stood behind her, his feathery head brushing the ceiling, his dark wings folded against his sides, but still filling the glass corridor completely. The weird, ambient light seemed to make the red of his eyes glow like fire.

Around its neck, hanging from a gold link chain, hung a shiny brass key.

It made a noise, something close to a chuckle, and clicked its beak at her. Penny shrieked, and ran.

As blind panic took over, Penny lost all sense of reason and direction. She ran until one mirror or another mocked her progress, forcing her into various side corridors, or sometimes back the way she'd come. She didn't scream, but only because she couldn't spare the breath for it.

The Birdman was always close, sometimes behind her in the twisting mirrored hallways, sometimes in the mirrors themselves. Once Penny felt the tickle of feathers against the back of her arm and clawed fingers scraping through her hair, but the sensation was gone quickly, and she put on a burst of speed that threatened to propel her through the next mirror she met.

Finally, she saw daylight and heard Zoe's screams as her friend emerged from a seemingly solid mirror surface just ahead and to the left of her. A moment later Rooster emerged from the right, his pudgy arms squashing his Stetson to his chest, his eyes popped open wide, and his chubby face twisted in a silent scream.

Then they were out, bursting through the open door at the end of the House of Mirrors like projectiles from the barrel of a gun, smashing into each other and the railing beside the stairs to the grass, seeing the pointing fingers of the people waiting below them in line, hearing their amused laughter, and not caring one bit.

Penny was just happy to be out of there. She had no idea of what she had hoped to accomplish with the trip. Maybe simple curiosity had coaxed them inside. She decided that nothing in the world would coax her back in.

Watching Rooster run away sobbing in terror lifted Penny and Zoe's moods a little as they left the House of Mirrors behind. However, Penny could not deny the occasional nervous glance back, just to make sure The Birdman hadn't flown out to catch her.

There were more screams from behind as more kids exited the House of Mirrors. Screams laced with nervous, tittering laughter, and Penny turned again to see the small group of boys clustered around the exit head straight to the back of the line again.

And why wouldn't they? It was scary, but fun, *if* you didn't know the truth about it. If you didn't know The Birdman chasing you through those mirrored hallways was real.

Susan was surprised when they asked to go home early, but she obliged, dropping them off at the top of the driveway before turning around for town again. Susan was opening the shop for a half day, which she did every Sunday during Harvest Days, and after that she and Jenny were going to spend some time enjoying the fair.

"I'll call about seven to check on you, so you better be

inside." Then she settled back in her seat, regarding them with curiosity for a moment. "Where is it you go all the time, anyway?"

Zoe squirmed a little.

"We have a place up at the edge of the field, in the trees," Penny said, referring to a grove of old, tall pines that stood where the wild field ended and the wilder hills began. A place far away from Aurora Hollow. "We like to go there because Rooster doesn't."

Susan waved as she drove away, and Penny waved back.

"I'm starved," Zoe said, and they went inside to pack bag lunches to take with them.

On the walk to the hollow, Zoe asked, "How long do you think she'll be gone?"

"Dunno," Penny said around a mouthful of sandwich. She chewed ferociously and swallowed before continuing. "She never goes out."

"We have to wait until she comes home and goes to sleep before we can go out tonight," Zoe said. "If she catches us out when we shouldn't be she'll probably ground us."

"But we do have to go tonight," Penny said. "He won't come for us while his ride is open. He has to work."

They scrambled down the steep bank. The dirt path, untouched for years until they found it, and now trodden daily, was getting loose and unreliable. Penny lost her footing halfway down, but Zoe grabbed her arm before she could tumble.

"We need to put stairs in," Zoe said. "You're a clumsy little thing."

"Har, har," Penny said. "You're a laugh a minute."

Penny and Zoe spent the afternoon practicing, getting better at Zoe's new spell, and Penny experimented with the shock spell, making it powerful enough to send her stuffed bear, now almost unrecognizable, several feet into the air. Smoke trickled from a hole where Penny zapped it, and she had to stomp out a tongue of flame that rose from the stuffing.

"Handy," Zoe said, looking honestly impressed.

Penny was less excited about it. She guessed it was almost as powerful as your garden-variety stun gun, but you had to be right up close for it to work, and she didn't want to get that close to The Birdman. That close he wouldn't have to use magic against them, just lift them into the air and fly away with them.

They lost track of time as they usually did in the hollow and had to run home. They were a few minutes late, and Penny snatched the ringing phone from its cradle, puffing and out of breath.

"There you are," Susan said sounding partly amused, partly exasperated.

"Sorry," Penny said in a croak. "We were outside."

"Time to stay in now. It's getting dark."

Penny could hear a chorus of laughing voices and huckstering from game booths on the other end of the line.

"Still at the fair?"

"Still here," Susan confirmed. "I borrowed Jenny's cell phone. I'm going to stay a while longer."

"How much longer?" Penny wondered if she and Zoe could risk another trip to the hollow before Susan returned for the night.

"A few more hours at least. The sheriff's making a

press release later tonight, and I'll probably stay in town for a bit afterward."

"The sheriff?" Penny was a little disquieted by this pronouncement. Knowing who, what, they were up against, Penny was doubtful the sheriff had come any closer to solving the mystery or finding the kids. Any progress he had to report was likely false progress, misleading, and maybe even dangerous. "What's it about?"

"Don't know," Susan said. "If it's anything important I'll give you a call."

Penny and Zoe decided to stay home for the rest of the night, and try to spend at least a few hours not worrying about The Birdman.

If they had known what news the sheriff was about to share with the town, they may have decided differently.

Chapter 18

The Truth about Tovar

Penny and Zoe kept their mirrors in the backpack with their wand and the remainders of the lunch they had packed earlier in the day. After opening the bag to stow her coat in it, Zoe dropped it near the recliner in the living room and sat down to watch television.

She didn't notice the bag tip over as her chair rocked against it. She didn't see one of the mirrors spill out onto the carpet.

She didn't see the dark, sleek head that passed into it, blood red eyes glowing as they darted around, searching, then finding the girl sitting oblivious, dozing to the images of an old sitcom rerun.

The thing's beak split in the parody of a smile, then faded.

Zoe heard a tap against the front door and snapped awake. Her first thought was that Penny had accidentally locked herself outside, but even as she rose, Zoe remembered her going up to her room to change while Zoe sat channel surfing and finding nothing worth watching. Sunday night television was, as a rule, lame.

Someone outside tried to turn the knob, but it only rattled. They'd locked it when they came back, had even used the door chain just to satisfy the paranoia that had been a part of life since Jodi Lewis's disappearance.

Zoe paused halfway across the living room, suddenly scared for no reason she could pin down.

It's just Susan, she thought. *She's come home early after all.*

A metallic snick sounded, and a moment later, the doorknob turned.

Zoe moved forward again to undo the chain, then froze for a second time. This time her fear had a face—a black, feathery face with a wicked, sharp-looking beak and burning eyes.

The door stopped at the end of its chain, but it was open far enough to admit one clumsy looking talon of a hand at the end of an arm that looked like crow's feathers glued to a stick. Beyond the leering bird face and reaching arm was a view Zoe could not immediately explain: not the darkness beyond Penny's front porch, but a large and dimly lit cavern.

Two of the cave's walls were clothed in scarlet tapestries that flapped and fluttered with some unfelt breeze. Candle flames likewise danced from the surface of a table in the center of the cavern. The table was not wood, but a dark gray stone polished to a gemstone shine.

"Penny!"

Zoe stumbled back a step, thinking of the wand tucked in her backpack somewhere behind her, but she could not turn. Her eyes were pinned helplessly on the monstrosity reaching up along the partially open door.

The Birdman's clawed fingers grasped the door chain and ripped it free of door and wall.

The door crashed open, affording Zoe with a full view of

the room on the other side, the room where no room should be, and she remembered it from their expedition the previous day. It was one of the locked and secret rooms in the House of Mirrors that Penny had viewed through a keyhole and later described to Zoe. The room that was too large to fit inside the trailer.

One of the tapestries fluttered, and she saw the kids lying on the floor behind it, stretched out in the relaxed poses of the deeply sleeping. Not just the four kids whose disappearance had caused such a panic in Dogwood, but a dozen or more, laid out side by side.

"Penny, help!"

Zoe heard Penny's answering shout, too far away.

The Birdman rushed forward, snapping its beak at her, its eyes fixed on hers.

She tried to look away, but could not. Even as the room around her began to fade and she felt her knees buckle, her neck craned and her eyes stayed on his. She heard the thump of her body against the hard wood floor of the living room, but the expected pain did not come. Her whole body was numb.

The gray fog became darkness, but it was not yet the darkness of unconsciousness. It was the darkness of huge black-feathered wings unfolding over her.

Penny was pulling her pajama top over her head when Zoe screamed from below.

"Zoe?"

She heard the front door crash open, then Zoe's wordless shriek.

She ran for the open trapdoor from her attic bedroom to the hallway below, still struggling to pull her shirt down. She tottered over the edge for a moment, trying to free her hands from the leather chord and the Phoenix Key hanging around her neck. Now that they kept the book locked inside the trunk while they were away, Penny never went anywhere without the key. By the time she'd untangled herself and started down the sliding stairs, Zoe's cries had regressed to mere babble, like the frightened half-talk of someone caught in a horrible dream.

Penny pounded down the upstairs hallway, bare feet slapping the floor painfully, and slid to a stop at the landing, grabbing hold of the handrail leading down the stairs.

There, she saw what she had feared.

The Birdman darted through the open front door, wings twitching and flaring up as if it wanted to fly away and had to restrain itself. Zoe hung from one of his arms, her sneaker-clad feet dragging on the floor and bumping over the threshold.

"No!"

The Birdman turned its horrible head and looked back at her over one shoulder. "I'll come back for you." Its voice was a high-pitched squawk, the voice of a trained parrot turned mean.

One clawed hand reached behind it and gripped the door, and before it swung shut Penny saw the room beyond, the room that shouldn't have been there at all: walls with fluttering red tapestries and a stone table supporting perhaps a hundred flickering candles. On the far side of the strange room, standing before a stone wall that looked natural rather than man-made, was a door with an inscribed brass knob and key plate.

This was the room she'd spied through a keyhole in the House of Mirrors.

She scrambled down the steps and lunged for her front door, but it slammed shut before she could reach it.

When Penny opened it again, there was only the dark of

night and a slightly overgrown yard beyond the front porch.

In a flash of intuition, Penny understood the business with the doors. The door in the hollow, how it had come to be there, and why. The strange doors in the House of Mirrors, and how the rooms glimpsed on the other side of them seemed too large to be contained in a simple trailer. She understood Zoe's story about her first encounter with The Birdman, who had seemed to materialize inside her closet, and she understood why it hadn't come for her.

There were no upright doors in her room for him to come through, just the small trapdoor in the floor.

Penny ran to Zoe's backpack and spilled its contents onto the floor. She plucked her wand from the pile, and the small mirror lying next to it, and ran back to the front door. Still dressed in her pajamas, she slipped on her shoes, bolted outside, and ran through the dark. Half convinced The Birdman would drop from the sky at any moment to bear her away, she ran with all her speed toward Aurora Hollow.

She had no doubt The Birdman would come for her, and probably soon. When he did, she wanted to face him on her own terms, and at the door of *her* choosing.

As summer in Dogwood glided into fall, the winds that often swept the town intensified and grew cold teeth.

Penny beat her frantic pace over the high field to the hollow, and the wind gusted up stronger, pushing at her back as if it wanted to pick her up and throw her into the clearing. She stumbled, almost fell, saw the treetops emerging from the creek canyon, and skidded to a halt at the edge. The wind gusted again, threatening to push her over, then it stilled.

Penny half slid, half ran down the crumbling trail,

brandishing her wand before she even hit the bottom. Flames exploded from the stone ring, rising a dozen feet into the air, licking at a few stray boughs, then dropped down to a normal level.

Penny ran past the fire, stopped in front of the door, and faced it.

The Birdman would come soon, and Penny only hoped she could handle him alone when he did.

But what if she didn't have to face him alone?

She closed her eyes and conjured up the image of Tovar, her father, red hair standing like frozen flames above his narrow and freckled face, smiling up at her from the mirror.

When she opened them again, she stared down into the mirror and said, "Father."

For a few seconds her own reflection stared back up at her. Then, like last time, her image faded in a fog, and Tovar's face appeared in its place. Like last time, he seemed surprised to see her, but his shock quickly changed to one of curious amusement.

"I need your help," Penny said, not sure if he could hear her or not, but knowing she had to try.

When the amusement dropped from his features, his eyebrows, red as his hair, red as hers, lifted in surprise.

"Can you come here?" Penny asked.

He watched her for a few more seconds, then nodded. His voice sounded through the mirror, muted, but clear. "Yes, little lady. I'm on my way."

His image darkened, faded, vanished.

A metallic click drew Penny's eyes up to the door, and she watched the knob turn, then, with a squall of rusted hinges, it swung open and Tovar The Red stepped through into Aurora Hollow. A cloak hung over his broad shoulders hiding his arms, the hem drifting down to his scuffed boots. Light from the open doorway behind him outlined him like an aura.

She saw him standing there, only a few feet away, and a jumble of emotions too complex to sort out swept her current worries away. She forgot about Zoe. She forgot about The Birdman. She forgot about Susan, who would return home soon to find the front door standing open, the lock chain torn loose, and both the girls gone. She could not speak. She couldn't even move.

"Never in my life," Tovar said, his voice colored by the same unidentifiable accent as Ronan's, "would I have expected to face you here, like this. There were rumors..."

His voice broke off, and he looked at her, his eyes, green like hers, narrowed a little. "What is your name?"

For a moment, Penny couldn't answer him, and when she did find her voice, it was dry, and almost as rusty as the hinges of the door.

"Penny," she said, and her paralysis broke.

She rushed forward then, wand clutched and forgotten in one hand, the mirror in the other, and threw her arms around him.

Tovar did not return the embrace, only stood stiffly looking down at her, his fiery eyebrows arched in mild surprise.

Standing there, with her arms thrown around the man she had just called father, she looked into the open doorway, and felt herself go cold, as if her blood had turned to ice water.

She looked through the door and into a hallway, one she had explored with Zoe the day before. It was a narrow hallway lined with doors, and she was looking in through one of them.

She released him and stepped away. She was once again aware of the wand in her hand, held at her side. She lifted it, pointing it at him.

"Who are you?"

Tovar's mild surprise bloomed into a good-humored grin.

"Little Princess Penny," he said in a singsong voice. "How have I vexed thee so?"

"Are you my father?" Her voice rose to a near shout, and the wand began to shake in her hand.

Tovar regarded her, regarded the shaking wand in her hand, and his good humor departed.

"It was a fine fantasy while it lasted, wasn't it, young Penny?"

She saw something shift under his cloak, and shouted. "Don't move!"

The rustling beneath his cloak stopped, but the expression on his face was supremely unconcerned. "A challenge, is it? Very good! Playing the part of the benign entertainer was getting old."

His cloak flew out behind him, as if thrown by a strong breeze, though there was none. Beneath it, he wore his simple white shirt, only half buttoned. A key swung from a chain around his neck.

Before she could react, his wand was up, pointing at her.

There was no time to throw a spell, so she dove to the side. Something that looked like a ghostly red skull flew past her. It smashed into the tree behind where she had stood, and she watched as its trunk withered and cracked, its limbs drooped, some snapping under their own weight, and its leaves grayed and fell to dust.

"No, not wise at all, I suppose," Tovar said, as if he'd just been scolded. "They'll want you alive. Yes, I think they'll be very interested in you, young Penny."

Tovar muttered something in a language too strange to comprehend, and a purple fog rushed from the tip of his wand, shifting form—a giant purple bird, a vaguely human form with outstretched arms, a shapeless, vaporous blob—as it moved through the air toward her.

Raising her wand from where she lay on the ground, Penny used the first spell that came to mind. She conjured a wind, focusing it on the approaching purple mass, forcing it back toward Tovar.

Tovar merely grinned wider at her through the poisonous-looking purple fog, unconcerned. When the fog had retreated to within a foot of him, he touched his wand tip to it, and it flashed like a flame and sizzled away to nothing.

"You do know a thing or two," he said, and laughed. "This is going to be fun."

His grin vanished when Penny sent a half-dozen burning red sparks at him. He waved his wand in a quick circle before him, and her sparks exploded into flames against an invisible shield.

Penny staggered to her feet, raising her wand again and waiting for the flames to clear. When they did, and the distorting shimmer of the shield he'd placed in front of himself faded, his good humor was gone. The expression on his face was something like anger. Before anger though, Penny thought she'd seen surprise. Maybe even uncertainty.

"You're not that good, Little Red," he said, and sent a glowing arch of blue lightning at her.

The first fork missed her, striking the dead tree to her left. The second fork struck her in the chest, lifting her off her feet even as it sent bright pain through every part of her body.

A moment later, she hit the ground on her back, her clenched jaw jerking open in a scream of pain. She could feel randomly twitching muscles, could see her hair dancing as the last few stray volts left her.

Penny rolled onto her side, tried to push herself up, but her trembling arms would not support her weight. She dropped to the ground again, tears of pain and frustration making tracks across her dusty cheek. She tried to push herself again, and only succeeded in freeing her trapped right arm.

She watched Tovar's booted feet approach her, tried to turn her head to face him, but could not. She tried lifting her wand, but her arm only twitched uselessly in the dirt.

Then he stood over her, and when he spoke, the good humor had left his voice too.

"You have guts, I'll give you that, but The Phoenix Girls

never did know when to quit, and I can see you're following in their footsteps."

He took a final step forward, close enough for her to reach out and touch him were she able to lift her arms. She did manage to turn her face up to his. "What do you know about The Phoenix Girls?"

"I know more than you'd believe, little Phoenix Girl," he said with some of his old humor, good-natured on the surface, but with a thread of cruelty she'd missed before. Mostly it shone out through his eyes. Those green eyes.

So much like her own.

"But you didn't call me here to talk about that troublesome band of witches, did you? No, I believe you are curious about your father." He placed his hands on his hips and laughed.

"What do you know about my father?" Though her traitor muscles still trembled and twitched, she had enough strength to yell.

"Again," he said, "more than you would believe. I suppose I can tell you enough to whet your curiosity at least. I could tell you everything, but where's the fun in that? I like to leave people guessing."

He crouched down then, and Penny noted the wand in his hand, pointed downward and slightly behind him. He leaned in close to her, and his smile faded.

"Where your father is now, there is no coming back from."

This time when Penny tried to move her arm, it did cooperate. She thrust the tip of her wand up into his chest, and sent her spell at him with every ounce of fury she possessed.

There was a crack as loud as a pistol shot, and Tovar flew backward through the air, a small charred hole in his shirt where her wand had touched, leaving a fine tendril of smoke wafting upward. Sparks danced across the ends of his flame-like hair, between his fingertips, arched between his boots.

She saw the wand fall from his hand even as he flew through the open door into the secret hallway of the House of Mirrors, and she lunged for it. Her movements were still slow, jerky, but she reached the black wand, clutched it with her free hand, and rose on quivering legs.

Tovar lay, still as death, on the other side of the door.

Not dead, she thought, *just knocked out.*

Somewhere past him, on the other side of that open door, The Birdman held Zoe prisoner. Zoe and the other kids, she had no doubt.

Before she stepped through, she raised her wand and forced the hinge bolts out of their rusty sleeves. They fell to the dirt, and then the door itself tipped over, crashing to the ground in a puff of dust and leaves.

If she was going to go through that door, she wanted to make sure it would be open when she and Zoe came back.

If she and Zoe came back.

Taking a deep, steadying breath, Penny crossed the threshold from the hollow into The Birdman's lair.

Chapter 19

Flight of The Birdman

Penny considered the doors around her, then turned back to the one she'd just come through. Second on the right coming in from the emergency exit, the one Zoe had spied trees behind when she'd looked through the keyhole.

She'd seen her reflection in the first one. A mirror, but what kind of mirror?

Zoe and the rest of the kids were behind one of these doors, she was certain of it.

Now, how to open them?

Penny turned back to Tovar, still lying sprawled out next to the open door, and spied the golden glint of a chain around his neck. She stuck his black wand into the waistband of her pajamas, pointed hers at him, giving it a quick *come to me* flick.

Tovar's key, smaller than her Phoenix Key, old and tarnished, slipped from underneath his cloak, pulling the chain tight as it tried to fly to her. Another flick of her wand and the chain quivered, tightened, then snapped. It flew into the palm of her waiting hand.

"Gotcha!" Penny jammed the key into the closest keyhole,

twisted it, and resisted the urge to cheer when the lock clicked.

She twisted the doorknob and pushed it open. A quick scan revealed a large and empty room furnished with antique-looking furniture, every wall draped with scarlet tapestries.

Next, and more out of a wild, irresistible curiosity than any real hope of finding anything, Penny opened the door behind which Zoe had seen her reflection. There was no room behind that one, but a mirror standing the length and depth of the opening. This mirror had a wet, swimmy look to it, as if it were made of a sheet of standing water rather than glass. Penny found herself wanting to reach out and touch it, and forced her hand back to her side.

The next door opened on a room not much larger than a closet, and after a moment she realized that's exactly what it was. Through rows of hanging robes, every color from scarlet, to green, to black, she spotted another door. She pushed her way through and grasped the plain brass doorknob. The door was unlocked, but opened on nothing.

As Penny turned to leave, she regarded the rows of hanging robes. After a brief hesitation, she riffled through them. It wouldn't be good for the other kids to recognize her if she did manage to find them. She found a red one. It was a little too large for her, but it would have to do. On her way through, she grabbed a green one that looked about Zoe's size and stuffed it into one of her robe's oversized pockets.

She opened other doors at random; one opened on what she thought was the inside of a cargo trailer stuffed with dismantled bleachers, a stage, and other props from Tovar's show. She realized she was looking out through the open door of the giant safe.

The next two doors opened on nothing at all, just black, open space that seemed to vibrate a faint, discordant hum.

These she slammed shut, not liking that hum or the possible horrors such an endless black space might hold.

The next door opened on a cavern, furnished with more of the hanging scarlet tapestries and a stone table covered with flickering candles, giving it the appearance of a secret, underground office—a place where unspeakable business is done and horrible deals made.

There was a door at the far end, standing feet away from a wall of solid stone. A large oval mirror hung on the front of the door, a mirror that at first glance appeared to be too filthy to reflect. As she ran toward it, Penny realized it was not filth, but a gray fog swirling in the interior.

Flickering candlelight glinted off something lying on the floor beside the door. A chain, Penny saw as she neared it. When she bent to examine it closer, she saw it was the lock chain from her own front door.

This is where he came through. This is where he brought Zoe!

This door had a plain doorknob, and there was nothing beyond it when she opened it but the room's stone wall.

The engraved doorknobs always go to the same place, she thought. *The ordinary doors go where you want.*

If she only knew how.

It didn't matter. She had to find Zoe.

Penny scanned the cavern again and saw no one. No sign at all that anyone might still be there. Just as she was ready to leave the cavern behind and search the next door, a faint ripple ran across a small section of tapestry to her left. Briefly, through a part in the curtain, she saw the cavern extended past that portion of tapestry.

Penny ran to it, very aware of how long this was taking. Also very aware that Tovar would awaken soon and come for her, and that The Birdman, who had not shown himself yet, could be anywhere.

Maybe even behind this, Penny thought, and hesitated with

a fold of the hanging cloth bunched in her fist. Feeling equal parts hope and fear, Penny at last yanked the tapestry aside, tearing it from the wall.

She found Zoe behind it, and for a moment, all thought drowned in the certainty that she was too late. Zoe, her best friend, was dead.

The cold hand that seemed to have gripped her heart slowly loosened. *Not dead,* she realized with a rush of relief. *Only sleeping.*

Stretched out across the dirt- and pebble-strewn ground as comfortable as a baby in a crib, and sleeping.

Beside Zoe, and around her, other kids also slept—and not just the four from Dogwood. Some Penny recognized, but most she didn't.

A loud snort from a boy nearby made her jump.

Penny ran to Zoe, knelt beside her, and gave her shoulder a shake.

"Zoe, wake up."

She knew it wouldn't work. The Birdman had put them into some kind of enchanted sleep only he would be able to break.

It did work.

Zoe's eyes popped open, and she seemed on the verge of screaming until she focused on Penny's face.

Resisting the urge to throw her arms around her friend, to shout with relief, Penny said, "Shhh, be quiet."

She pointed all around them, and Zoe followed her finger, seeing the others sprawled across the cavern floor.

"Put this on. Hide your face," Penny said, handing her the green robe.

For a moment Zoe only goggled, then she nodded, stood, and slipped the robe on. When it settled over her shoulders, she pulled the hood over her head.

Penny pressed Tovar's black wand into Zoe's hand and said, "We have to get them out of here, and quickly, before The Birdman comes back."

Zoe gaped at the wand in her hand, then faced Penny. "How?"

Penny pointed toward the open door back into the House of Mirrors trailer.

Zoe looked through, her eyes growing wider by the second. Then the look of disorientation left her face and she nodded.

They realized quickly that it *was* an enchanted sleep. The Harvest Day parade could have proceeded through the cavern full volume and they wouldn't have awakened. The key to breaking the enchantment was a simple one though.

"Katie," Penny whispered, grabbing Katie West's shoulder as she did so, and the girl's eyes flew open at the sound of her name. Penny was sure Katie had seen her face beneath her hood before she had backed away, and could only hope she wouldn't blab later.

Zoe had already awakened the other three town kids, but the others remained deaf to them.

"We're going to have to carry them," Zoe said.

Penny groaned, then nodded.

Penny went out first, peering cautiously through the open door, first one way, then the other, to see who might be waiting for them.

No one was waiting for them, but she was far from relieved.

Tovar was gone. He had awakened and escaped. Or

maybe his feathery friend had carried him away. Someone had closed the mirror door, and Penny could almost picture Tovar walking through it, the reflective surface parting around his shape to admit him, then closing when he was through.

She had no doubt at all he was somewhere close, maybe hiding, but most likely watching and waiting.

There was nothing to do but go forward though, so she motioned to Zoe and Katie, who got the others moving in her direction.

Penny moved into the hallway, half carrying, half dragging the youngest of the sleeping kids, a girl a few years younger than she was, but only a little smaller. She moved slowly and kept her wand pointed ahead, just in case. Katie followed her, struggling under the weight of another sleeping kid slung over her shoulder. The oldest girl, the one who'd sprouted flowers during Tovar's first show, carried one of the young twins from Auburn over each shoulder. The boy followed her, moving easily under his cargo. Zoe was last, grunting under the dead weight of a sleeping boy, her wand also out and ready to use.

The door at the end of the hall, the one that led nowhere but outside, was locked, and Tovar's key didn't fit it.

Penny cursed under her breath and stepped away from the door. She'd hoped to avoid this, but she wasn't strong enough to break the door down, so she had no choice.

Holding her wand so the others could not easily see it, she pointed it at the door and blasted it open.

The sound was like a gunshot in the enclosed corridor, eliciting shocked cries from behind her. The door buckled and flew off its hinges, landing with a muffled crash outside.

The view beyond the door was perhaps the sweetest sight Penny had ever seen, the dark green of moonlit grass and the lazily moving water of the river.

Penny led them around the House of Mirrors and through the deserted park, winding through the games, rides, and booths until she reached the tree at the edge of the park, the one she'd seen Zoe reading under on her first trip into town. She dropped to the grass, relieving herself of the sleeping girl's weight.

When they had all arrived, Katie opened her mouth to speak.

Penny shook her head and put a finger to her lips. "Don't tell anyone."

Disguising her voice as well as she could, Penny pointed at Katie. "Go to the Sheriff's Office and tell them to come back here."

Penny turned to the oldest girl and the boy, startling them back a step. "You two stay here and wait."

"Let's get out of here," Zoe whispered, and Penny nodded.

They ran back to the House of Mirrors, jumped the back fence, and sprinted through the blasted back door.

Zoe stopped at the open door to the hollow, but Penny restrained her, grabbing the back of her robe.

"We can't yet."

"What?"

"They," Penny paused for a second, not wanting to say the name, but knowing she had to. "Tovar and The Birdman used the mirrors to find people. They use these doors to kidnap them and get away."

Zoe nodded. "Okay then. Let's make sure they can't use them again."

Little as either wanted to, they made their way back to the cavern door.

"That's the one," Penny said, pointing to the big oval mirror on the door. "He used it to look through our little mirrors to find us." She stepped through, back into the cavern, and ran to the door. Zoe followed, and when Penny bent down to pick up the door chain to her front door, Zoe nodded.

"Yeah," Zoe said, and moved in front of the door, turning to view the cavern from this new perspective. "This is the room I saw when he took me."

Penny dropped the door chain into her robe's pocket, stepping back from Zoe's raised wand.

After a few moments Zoe lowered her wand, frowning. "It's not working."

Penny raised hers, pointing it at the mirror, preparing to shatter it into a million glittering pieces.

Her wand would not respond. There was not even the fizzle or pop that usually meant she wasn't focused enough.

After a moment's debate, she grabbed the oval mirror and lifted it from its hook on the door. Carrying it under one arm, she followed Zoe through the cavern door.

"What now?" Penny wondered aloud.

Zoe considered the question for a moment, then she raised the black wand, pointed it toward the dead end of the corridor, where it led deeper into the House of Mirrors, and when she tried the black wand again, it did work. She sent a fat, boiling fireball flying down the hallway. A second later the hallway was in flames, and they ran toward the exit. The flames followed them, rolling across the floor like a wave.

Penny slid to a stop short of the exit and grabbed Zoe's sleeve, yanking her to a stop.

"What are you doing?" Zoe almost screamed.

"Through there," Penny said, pointing through the open doorway into the hollow.

They rushed through, and as Penny's feet hit the ground on the other side, elation lit her from within.

"We did it!"

Elation quickly gave way to panic as flames licked the empty doorframe, dancing through and reaching toward the lower boughs of the willows like the merry tongue of a demon.

Zoe shouted in shock, then frustration. "Where's the door?"

A second later, she spotted it and bent down, dropping Tovar's wand and digging her fingers into the dirt under its edge. She struggled with it, lifting her end several inches off the ground.

Penny helped by lifting it with her wand, and Zoe guided it back into the frame.

"Hold it!" Penny dropped to her knees in front of the door, searching for the hinge pins.

"Hurry up. It's getting too hot!"

Penny found the first, then the second a few inches away, and scrambled to the door on her hands and knees. She shot the first bolt into the bottom hinge, but was too short to reach the top.

Zoe snatched it from her hand and pushed it into the top hinge from the bottom. She shoved the door shut, and when the latch tongue clicked in place, the door began to cool almost at once. The orange glow of flames licking between the top of the door and the frame winked out.

Zoe did not relax with the closing of the strange door, but snatched the black wand from the ground and retreated a few steps. "He can still come through."

"No, he can't," Penny said, and when Zoe turned to regard her, she pulled his key from her pocket. "He needs this."

"Are you sure?"

"Pretty sure," Penny said.

"Very well done, young ladies," said a voice from the

trees. "I would indeed need that key to come back through. Luckily for me, I'm already here."

Penny and Zoe turned in unison to the sound of Tovar's voice, both raising their wands. They fired identical spells at the red magician, but before either could reach him, giant black wings spread from his shoulders, pushing his cloak out behind him. He crouched and leapt, his wings pumping the air, and shot straight up through the trees.

Their spells passed below his feet, blasting leaves from the hanging willow limbs.

"Where'd he go?" Zoe spun in a circle, searching.

"I don't know!" Penny searched the sky above them, saw a dark shape pass across the moon, then lost track of it.

They both screamed when something crashed through the green canopy over their heads. A moment later, one of Tovar's boots landed in the dirt between them.

They both stared at it.

Tovar dropped from the night sky screaming, and Penny saw his feet, bootless bird's talons, clenching and unclenching on empty air before one of them grabbed the back of Zoe's shirt and the other snatched the wand from her hand.

Zoe shrieked as Tovar rocketed upward through the overhead boughs, then dropped her, and before Penny could even think to raise her wand to help, Tovar, The Birdman, plummeted downward again. He caught Zoe a bare moment before she would have crashed to the ground, pinning her against him, a human shield, and pointed his recovered wand at Penny.

Penny did not lower hers. If she did Tovar would capture her too, and any chance they had to escape him would be gone.

"You have been a lot of trouble, you little red monster! It's a familial trait, like your father's red hair, and those pretty green eyes." Tovar's face broke into a wide, handsome smile of good humor, but Penny knew that face was a lie, an illusion.

"You don't know anything about my father! Let her go," she shouted, taking a step forward, holding her wand steady. She did not attack though, as much as she wanted to. She was afraid she'd hit Zoe.

Tovar broke into gales of artless, honest laughter, the laughter of a man with some inside joke he's bursting to share. "I know much. Much more than you, anyway. In fact, I don't think I've ever met a person so ignorant of their own history and heritage."

"I don't believe you!" She did though. She couldn't help but believe him.

Tovar shrugged, a grotesque gesture that sent his wings fluttering.

"Your belief or disbelief matters not a bit. But if you require proof, you could always ask the woman you called mother when you meet her in the next life."

He winked at her, and Penny found herself wanting nothing more than to blast that smile off his face.

"The woman who called herself Diana Sinclair was not who she claimed to be. I'm not altogether sure *she* knew who she was anymore."

The smile faded from his face, and he fixed her with his cold green eyes. Not his real eyes, only part of the mask he wore, but his real eyes would be just as cold.

"However, you'll have all the answers you could hope for on the other side. I'll not return empty-handed."

He twitched his wand upward, and Penny felt her own try to leap from her hand. She tightened her grip on it, using both hands to keep it from flying away. The force pulling it strengthened for a moment as Tovar pulled his wand upward, then disappeared as he relented.

Penny sent a blast of air at him, throwing his cloak out behind him like a black flag, catching his unfurled wings and throwing him off balance before he could tuck them back at his sides.

Tovar laughed. "Is that all you've got, little one?" He gave his wand a minute wave, a tight little circle.

The world seemed to twist in Penny's vision, and a wave of nausea crashed down on her. Her knees came unhinged, and the pain that shot up her legs as they hit the hard, stony earth seemed unimportant in the face of the terror and confusion that suddenly held her. The earth itself tried to buck her off, and she fell face first to the ground, digging her fingers into the dirt as the world twisted, rolled, and tried to send her tumbling in all directions at once. All sense of balance, of up and down deserted her. Earth and sky swapped places, and she felt gravity itself rejecting her.

The sound of Tovar's laughter pierced her terror like a needle, and a sudden, growing anger gave her a fraction of her focus back. She turned her face up, fighting a renewed nausea, and saw Tovar tracing complex patterns in the air before him. He finished with a sharp downward slash of his wand, and a bright purple line appeared in front of him.

It crackled, buzzed, glowed brighter, and opened like a vertical mouth in the air. Through it, Tovar and Zoe's shapes were dim, almost not there at all.

Penny pushed herself up with trembling hands, could not quite gain her feet, and so knelt before the stretching, widening crack in reality, balancing herself on one hand and raising her wand with the other.

"Run, Penny," Zoe cried, struggling fruitlessly against the arm pinning her to Tovar's chest.

Tovar turned his attention back to Penny.

"They'll want you alive, I suppose, but I don't think

they'll care if you're damaged," and with a snarl, he brandished his wand at her.

Without thinking, Penny forced her wand up, and parried his spell with one of her own.

The shield shimmered between them for only a few seconds before her concentration broke and she spilled back to the dirt, but it was long enough. Penny saw his spell fly toward her, shining and opalescent in the firelight. It struck her shield, bowing it in as if determined to break through, then rebounded back on him.

The spell hit Tovar in the face, snapping his head back, knocking the wand from his raised hand, and she saw smoke rise from the singed and reddening skin of his hand.

His face, the false face of Tovar The Red, sizzled and burned away, and the dark, slick feathers and snapping beak of his true face appeared.

Tovar screeched, the cry of a wounded monster bird, and lunged for the doorway he'd drawn, dragging Zoe behind him.

Zoe punched, clawed, kicked, but could not break his hold.

"No," Penny said, clawing the ground to drag herself forward, still held in the clammy grip of vertigo and nausea.

The sound of a low growl, something with a throat full of rage, drew her attention, making her skin prickle with a fresh wave of fear.

Then she saw him, crouched in his hole on the other side of the creek. His red fur bushed up, his snout wrinkled up to show snarling rows of sharp little teeth.

"Let go of her you dirty crow," Ronan growled, and leapt across the water. He rebounded off the trunk of the tree at the water's edge and flew at Tovar, scrambling up the smoldering black cape, sinking his teeth into the back of the monster's neck.

Screeching in fresh pain, Tovar released Zoe and clawed at Ronan, catching him by his bushed out hackles, and threw him.

Before Penny's chin hit the ground and she lost consciousness, she saw Zoe shove Tovar toward that glowing fissure he'd drawn between them.

Tovar The Red, The Birdman, tumbled through it, his screams fading like the scream of something falling down a long well.

The glowing lines closed into a single vertical line again, then burned out, and he was gone.

Penny fainted.

Chapter 20

Unanswered Questions

Penny awoke to a tug on her arm, and the pressure of sharp teeth pinching her flesh. She didn't want to wake up. She was comfortable, the residual pain from the spells that had hit her was fading, and the world was no longer spinning out of control, swapping earth and sky, trying to buck her off.

"Nuh-huh," she mumbled, pushing against the furry muzzle that closed on her arm.

The teeth let go of her arm, but continued tugging on the sleeve of her robe.

"Come on, Little Red. You have to go." The voice, muffled slightly by a mouthful of cloth, was familiar and welcome. She wanted to ask Ronan where he'd been, she hadn't seen him for weeks, but the desire to sleep was stronger. She'd ask him later.

"Penny, wake up!"

She felt hands on her shoulders, lifting her from the ground, supporting her in an uncomfortable sitting position—and the last scraps of a happy dream, one where her father came to help her get rid of The Birdman, slid away. Penny opened her eyes.

She saw Zoe, still holding her shoulders, Tovar's black wand stuck in the waistband of her jeans. Her pale, frightened face relaxed a bit. Sitting next to her, Ronan barked in excitement and leapt into Penny's lap, bathing her cheek with wet licks.

The last of her lingering confusion departed. Penny remembered where they were, and what had happened.

They had done it, faced Tovar, not The Red, but The Birdman, and won.

Penny pulled Ronan close with one arm, dragged Zoe down, and hugged her with the other.

"We did it," she said, as much to herself as the others.

"Yeah," Zoe said. She sounded almost as shocked as Penny felt.

"You did well, young ladies," Ronan said. "Very well, but it's time for you to go now, before Susan finds you missing."

Zoe broke from Penny's arms and pulled her to her feet.

Ronan scrambled off her lap and ran up the steep path, waiting for them at the top. "Get that mirror. We need to get you two back home. Hurry, there's no time to waste."

Zoe dashed back to the closed door, stooping to pick up the mirror they'd taken from Tovar's lair.

Penny expected the vertigo and nausea to return when she moved, but it did not. She ran up the hill to Ronan's side, and a few moments later Zoe came up behind them.

While Zoe made her way down the trail, Penny knelt beside Ronan.

"Where have you been? We really missed you…and who was that? How did he know so much about me?"

Ronan moved closer to her, his furry snout only a few inches away from her face.

"I cannot say, but you shouldn't dwell on anything that trickster told you. His kind are liars and thieves." He was silent for a moment, peeking down the dark trail toward Zoe, who stood waiting. "Yet...he was familiar with this place…you've seen how well he disguised himself. He's been here before."

"But why?" Penny reached out, hesitated, and put a hand on Ronan's shoulders. She had to resist the urge to pet him like a dog.

She somehow knew that would irritate him. "Why would he come here? Why was he trying to kidnap us?"

"To sell as slaves," Ronan said without hesitation. "Where he comes from, human children bring a high price."

"He was going to sell us?" Zoe, tired of waiting alone in the dark, had joined them again. Her normally dark skin was pale in the moonlight.

"Children can be trained…conditioned to forget freedom." Ronan looked away from them, then slipped from beneath Penny's hand and started down the trail again. "We have to go now."

They ran to catch up, Penny replaying Ronan's words in her head. She did not entirely trust his answer.

I cannot say did not necessarily mean *I don't know.*

As they ran, the aches of the night's work began to settle into Penny's bones and muscles again, and the questions continued to gnaw at her.

How did he know so much about her?

How did he know about her mother?

How did he know about her father?

They arrived to find the house still deserted, the phone ringing.

For the second time that night, Penny rushed to pick it up. "Susan?"

Susan's voice blared from the speaker, not angry, but excited, and Penny had to hold the phone away from her ear.

"No. We were upstairs…what?" She turned to Zoe and

pointed at the television. "Yeah, we're turning it on."

Zoe seemed frozen in place, but a nudge from Ronan got her moving. She knelt in front of the TV and turned it on. Canned laughter filled the living room.

"Find the news."

Zoe flipped through channels until she found the local station, broadcasting live.

"Yeah, okay." Penny hung up and turned toward Zoe and Ronan, who lay curled up in front of the television. "She'll be home soon."

Penny recognized the scene on the screen in front of them. It was the park, bathed by the light of dancing flames and the red strobes of fire engine lights. The giant effigy of The Birdman was wreathed in flames and tilting crazily as the House of Mirrors fell in on itself.

The camera panned on the perky, smiling face of a local reporter.

"...Engulfed in flames, while its owner, the magician known as Tovar The Red, is being sought in connection with the kidnapping of over a dozen children. The children remember almost nothing of their ordeal, except for their miraculous rescue from The House of Mirrors by two mysterious robed figures..."

Penny immediately pulled her pilfered robe off, and Zoe followed suit.

Ronan sprang to his feet and spun around to face them.

"...Local authorities speculate that the children may have been put into trances by Tovar, an accomplished hypnotist..."

"Were you seen?" Ronan turned his gaze from one to the other, his eyes wide and his posture tense.

Penny shot Zoe a guilty sideways look.

"You were," he said, almost barked. For the first time since they'd met him, he sounded truly angry.

"...statewide manhunt for this real life boogeyman, and

the community of Dogwood rejoices tonight as its children are once again safe in the arms of their loving families. Coming only minutes after Sheriff Price's press conference announcing the release of Gregory Hicks, whose name was cleared after an alibi witness came forward…"

The giant birdman effigy collapsed, sending glowing embers into the night sky.

So that's what the press conference was about, Penny thought.

Penny reached down and turned the television off.

"We hid our faces, but I think Katie West recognized us."

Zoe nodded. "I know she did."

Ronan sat in front of them, his bushy tail curling around his forepaws. "Will she tell?"

Penny wanted to say no, wanted to believe Katie would reward her rescue with discretion, but just didn't know.

Ronan seemed to guess that, and though he didn't look happy about it, he spoke more kindly. "You did the right thing. You saved those children from lives of misery and enslavement, but you must be careful. No one can know. If the rest of them find out about you, The Phoenix Girls will be finished."

Zoe stared at him, her mouth working as if searching for a reply.

"That book says we're supposed to find more…more like us," Penny said. "How are we supposed to do that if we can't tell anyone?"

"You are, but only when you're sure about them. You must be able to trust them as you would a sister." He stalked between them, heading for the hallway and the open front door. "This isn't a game. You have a serious purpose."

"What is it then?" Penny followed Ronan into the hall. "Why is it? If it's so serious, tell us what we're supposed to be doing!"

Ronan turned to regard her again, but chose not to

answer.

"How do we know when we've found the right person?"

"When you've found the right person, you will know," Ronan said. "How about this Katie?"

Penny and Zoe faced each other, Zoe actually grinning, though a little sourly.

"I don't think so," Penny said.

"Not a chance," Zoe said.

Ronan shrugged, a very human gesture, Penny thought. "Then you better hope she's grateful enough to keep your secret."

He regarded them for a moment more, then flashed his toothy grin. "You girls are full of questions, and you'll have all the answers you'll ever want—when the time for answers comes."

He sprang through the open door and vanished into darkness. His voice, fading into the distance, called back to them a final time. "For now, just be proud of what you've accomplished. You've had quite enough excitement for one night."

"Furry little pain in the butt," Zoe said, but with a smile. She walked back to the living room, and Penny heard the TV again.

Penny agreed. She'd had more than enough excitement for one night, but she thought sleep would be hard to find. Of all the questions Ronan *had* answered, it was the unanswered ones that continued to trouble her.

Chapter 21

The Third Phoenix Girl

Halloween night saw the streets of Dogwood overrun with trick-or-treaters, and though more adults than usual walked with them and stood guard at every street corner, there was no fear. Only the giddy, harmless frights of Halloween haunted houses and the usual assortment of kid-sized monsters.

Penny and Zoe were allowed to go around alone, as long as they returned to Sullivan's, which Susan had kept open late to hand out Halloween treats, every now and then.

This season's most popular costumes were robes, red and green mostly, worn in homage to the mysterious Dogwood witches who had gained an almost mythic status since the fair.

Though the stories behind the rescue varied wildly depending on whom you talked to, most agreed that the mysterious green and red clad rescuers were nothing more than childish fancy. The local kids had rallied around the myth and made it their own though.

Penny and Zoe did not wear red and green; they had

dressed for the night in the black dresses and pointed hats of the traditional Halloween witch.

They were confident that the only person in Dogwood who had recognized them that night had kept quiet about what she'd seen, but there was no need to push their luck.

And speaking of Katie West, their unlikely helper that night three weeks ago…

"Hey, Zoe." Penny nudged Zoe and nodded down the street toward a group of girls congregated around a tall stuffed man in red. An effigy of the magician, Tovar.

Some of the girls wore the red and green robes that were the season's fad. They took turns whacking the stuffed man in red with bats, laughing or crying out in an almost savage glee as they did so.

One girl stood apart from the others. She wore no costume at all, and seemed rather bored with the fun and games the others enjoyed. She watched Penny and Zoe as they approached, then with a last look back at her old friends, walked away.

The group she'd been with did not follow her, but only gave her the shortest of considerations before returning to their game.

Penny could see candy spilling from the red man's side where the latest blows had torn it open.

"Hey, little bro." A voice Penny recognized but couldn't immediately place startled her. "It's the little red monster and her faithful sidekick."

Penny and Zoe turned in unison to find Rooster and his older brother standing a few feet behind them. Rooster looked like a pint-sized race car driver in his white-and-red-striped leather pants and jacket. His helmet was too big for his head and tilted awkwardly to the left. It was white with red stars.

They could see only his eyes through the visor, but they were wide with amusement. "Even with your pathetic godmother giving away candy to half the kids in town you can't get anyone else to hang out with you."

"Don't seem to be fitting in too well," Rooster's brother said, false concern on his face. "It's a shame."

"Maybe you should hop on your brooms and fly away," Rooster said, chuckling.

Penny's right hand inched toward the opening of the candy bag in her left, toward her concealed wand.

Zoe nudged her with an elbow, and gave her head a barely perceptible shake.

Rooster saw this and laughed louder. "What're you gonna do, throw candy at me?"

New laughter joined, then drowned out Rooster's, and the four of them, Penny and Zoe, Rooster and his brother, turned to see who'd joined them.

It was Katie West, walking past the demolished and now abandoned piñata. She approached them with a casual stride, shaking with laughter.

Penny felt herself blush, felt tears of rage threaten to come spilling out. After everything they'd done, after saving her, this was how Katie repaid them?

Next to her, Zoe stiffened, and this time Penny had to grab her arm to keep her from grabbing her hidden wand.

Then Katie said something that made Penny's jaw drop.

"Look at you," she nearly doubled over with an intense burst of giggles, and pointed past Penny and Zoe, right at Rooster. "WiddleWeebleKniebel…all revved up and nothing to jump!"

Zoe's high, surprised laughter joined Katie's, and Penny turned to see Rooster's reaction.

He said nothing, his eyes narrowing behind the visor. The helmet slid a little further over his face, and then she could see only his nose and the sneering set of his upper lip.

Even his brother was speechless, though his cool and

disapproving glare shifted from Penny to Katie.

"Where's your widdlebikey?" Katie stopped between Penny and Zoe, finally giving in completely to her laughter. She gripped a handful of Penny's black witch's robe to keep from falling to her knees.

Penny's own laughter surprised her, and soon she was struggling to stay upright too,

"Shut up!" Rooster shouted from under his helmet. His voice was high-pitched with embarrassment and muffled.

The three girls burst into freshly renewed laughter, clutching each other awkwardly to stay on their feet.

"Oh … don't move Rooster. I need a picture of this." Katie pulled her cell phone from her jeans pocket, but before she'd opened it to take his picture, Rooster was running away.

His brother, tall, composed, intimidating, only smiled at them. It was a tight-lipped and humorless expression.

"That wasn't very nice, West. You should know better than that." He turned his chilly expression on Zoe and Penny in turn. "Don't get too comfortable in Dogwood, Little Red."

Then he turned and followed Rooster's rapidly retreating form.

When he'd turned the corner around the block, vanishing from their sight, the girl's laughter began to taper off. When it finally died out, Katie took a step back from Penny and Zoe, her eyes darting between them. The expression on her face was strange, almost alien, and Penny decided after a few seconds contemplation that it looked alien because, for the first time, it was anxious rather than scornful.

"Hi, Penny, Zoe."

"Hi," Penny said, still more wary than hopeful. This girl had hated her only a month before, and for nothing she had ever done.

Zoe said nothing, just stood back a step and watched Katie. Now that the laughter was over, her reflexive wariness of Katie had returned.

"Listen, I know it was you," Katie said, keeping her voice low.

Penny sighed and braced herself. This is what she'd been afraid of since that night in the park when Katie had seen her face beneath the hood.

"I'm sorry about..." she struggled with the apology, and the petty satisfaction Penny would have expected did not come.

"I won't tell anyone if you don't want me to. I'm sorry," she said again, then, "thanks."

Penny sighed again, this time in relief.

"It's okay," Zoe said. "Don't mention it."

"Yeah," Penny agreed. "Forget about it."

Katie's unease wilted slowly, and she smiled.

Then her eyes shifted down toward the sidewalk behind them, grew wide, shocked, and she slapped her hands over her mouth to stifle a scream.

Penny and Zoe spun, hands going instinctively for their hidden wands, and saw Ronan sitting behind them, grinning up at them and shaking his furry head from side to side.

"Why does everyone scream the first time they see me?"

Penny and Zoe shifted their gazes from Ronan, to Katie, to Ronan again, then looked at each other and smiled.

"It talks?" Katie asked in a weak voice.

Zoe laughed. "He does more than talk."

Penny smiled too, then laughed when Katie returned her smile with an uneasy one of her own.

All of the worries and questions about her long absent father and The Birdman's insinuations about her mother fled for a time, replaced by the simple joy of a new friendship, and the anticipation of adventures, and magic, yet to come.

The end...for now.

About Brian Knight

Brian Knight lives in Washington State with his family and the voices in his head. Brian has published over a dozen novels and novellas and two short story collections in the horror, dark fantasy, and crime genres. Several of his short stories have received honorable mentions in Year's Best Fantasy and Horror. *The Phoenix Girls Book 1 – The Conjuring Glass* is his first young adult work.

Photo by Judi Key

CPSIA information can be obtained at www.ICGtesting.com
Printed in the USA
LVOW08s2355161114

414028LV00001B/31/P